Love, Mates & Money

Kathryn Lamb lives quietly in Gillingham, Dorset, with her six children and five cats. Without the help of her family she would have found it a lot more difficult to write this book. She would like to thank them all, including some very special grandparents.

Kathryn draws cartoons for *Private Eye* and *The Oldie*. She has written and illustrated a number of books for Piccadilly Press, which have been published in many languages throughout the world (including Italian, German, Dutch, Thai, Russian and Korean!).

Other titles by Kathryn Lamb:

Boywatching!
The World According to Alex (Pick of the Year, Federation of Children's Book Groups Book of the Year Award – Longer Novel, 2000)
More of Everything According to Alex
The Last Word According to Alex
For Better or Worse According to Alex
Work, Rest and Play According to Alex
Summer, Sun and Stuff According to Alex
Honestly Mum!

Love, Mates & Money

Kathryn Lamb

Piccadilly Press • London

For Izobel, Gareth and Safia, with love

First published in Great Britain in 2005
by Piccadilly Press Ltd,
5 Castle Road, London NW1 8PR
www.piccadillypress.co.uk

A catalogue record for this book is available from
the British Library

ISBN: 185340 865 4 (trade paperback)

1 3 5 7 9 10 8 6 4 2

Printed and bound in Great Britain by Bookmarque Ltd
Cover illustration by Kathryn Lamb. Cover design by Fielding
Design. Text design by Textype, Cambridge.
Set in Soupbone, Regular Joe and Novarese.

Chapter 1

Natasha

WHY DO I LET MYSELF in for it?

Here I am *again* in Sophie's room at the end of a long, hot Tuesday spent slaving away at St Boris's Comprehensive (roll on the summer holidays — just four weeks away!), lending her my shoulder to cry on. (She needs to cry on it when she is in Major Crisis Mode, which happens about twice every week, on average.) Today's crisis involves a boy called Darren, in the year above us, who failed to return the dazzling smile that Sophie gave him as he passed by in the canteen. I point out that it may have had something to do with the chocolate bar that Sophie was eating at the time, and that maybe he was put off by the chocolate drool.

'I was *not* drooling! He just *hates* me!' she wails,

grabbing a handful of tissues to blow her nose and wipe away the tears.

'He doesn't hate you – and you *were* drooling! You always do when Darren's around.'

'I do not!' She gives me a friendly push, but she is smiling now. 'Do you *really* think he *doesn't* hate me?' Her blue eyes are shining, and her small, delicate, upturned nose with its light sprinkling of freckles is slightly less red than it was.

'Yes,' I say, with a sigh.

'That's a good start, isn't it – I mean, the fact that he doesn't *entirely* hate me? You're a good friend, Tash – you always cheer me up. Thanks!' She gives me a hug, her straight blond shoulder-length hair brushing against my cheek. (My hair is brown and frizzy with a tendency to grow out sideways – I spend a fortune on intensive hair conditioners.)

'It's OK,' I tell her. And it's true – I nearly always do manage to cheer Sophie up, which is a good feeling. I like being her best mate, the one she turns to in her hour, minute, second of need. I only get annoyed sometimes because of her tendency to switch to Major Crisis Mode at the slightest thing (we're talking Serious Drama Queen!). But – most of the time – we have a good laugh together, and we decided ages ago (in primary school!) that we'd be Best Mates Forever!

Sophie looks happy now, and picks up her

sketchbook and pencil to do some drawing. Her sketchbook is like a diary in pictures, and on the cover she has written 'Sophie's Sketchbook – Scenes from My Life'.

SOPHIE'S
SKETCHBOOK
SCENES FROM
MY LIFE
COOL! HI! SOPHIE

She is brilliant at drawing, although I wasn't sure about a picture she did of

MY BEST
MATE, TASH
(WHO HATES
THIS DRAWING!!!)

LEG WENT A
BIT WRONG

me – I looked like a stick insect with mad hair! (She told me the drawing went wrong, and I look much nicer than that!)

Sophie is sitting cross-legged beside me, while I lie back on her double bed. How I envy her the double bed! I have *always* wanted one, but Mum has been too busy on her laptop and her mobile, organising conferences – she runs a business called Conferences 4 U – to get round to replacing the kiddies' bed I have had forever, despite the fact that my arms and legs now hang off the end and sides . . .

Enjoying the sense of superiority that being the Wise Woman Who Speaks Words of Reassurance always gives me, I continue. 'And really, when you come to think of it, what will be, will be. Who knows what the future holds? For any of us . . . '

'I do,' says Sophie.

'What?'

'I have the gift.'

'Oh no – not this again! I know, I know. Your mum's psychic, and you've inherited her gift of second sight.'

'Well – I have! It's passed down from mother to daughter. So Kyle hasn't got it . . . ' Kyle is Sophie's brat of a twelve-year-old brother, two years younger than Sophie and me, whose main aim in life seems to be to annoy us as much as possible – at the moment, thankfully, he is out.

'So how come,' I muse, 'you failed to predict that I would get a detention in French? You might have warned me that our homework was due in today.'

'The gift only works for matters of the heart,' Sophie explains, condescendingly. It is her turn to be superior.

'I see. That figures – my heart wasn't really in my French homework.'

'But I can tell you one thing for certain,' says Sophie, looking miserable again. 'It's not going to work between me and Darren – I just *know* it. And my horoscope in *Lurve* magazine said that Jupiter is blocking my Lurve Curve. And if Darren's not part of it, I don't *have* a future.'

'Is that bad?'

'Very. And if Darren's – '

Oh no, here we go again. She's reaching for the tissue box – quick! Think of something!

'Stop! I mean . . . sorry for making you jump!' Sophie looks surprised, but I have her attention. 'I know what you need!'

'What? Darren?'

'No! Retail therapy! Like it says in your magazine.' I pick up the latest issue of *Lurve* magazine, which I have been idly flicking through. Sophie devours magazines like no one else I know. There are heaps of them under her bed, with names like *Teen Scene* and *My Mag*. Sophie laps up the horoscopes and problem pages. I don't believe in horoscopes, but I go along with the retail therapy advice. 'Let's hit the town! We'll go shopping at the mall on Saturday – we can go on the train. That'll cheer us up!'

'Great! There's just one teensy-weensy problem.'

'What's that?'

'No money.'

'Oh. Not even enough for the train fare to Bodmington Central?' (We live in Southway, a suburb of Bodmington.)

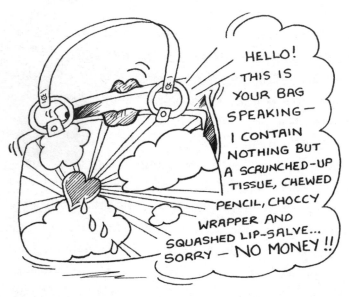

Sophie shakes her head. I do a quick mental calculation. 'Well, with the money I owe Mum for the last shopping trip, and the money I owe my darling sister for lending me enough to get that CD I wanted, I have . . .' I frown in concentration. '. . . exactly minus twenty-four pounds. I told Mum that some of it could come out of my next pocket money, and Kezia will have to wait. So Kezia *won't* be in a good mood, and she *won't* give us a lift in her car – it's broken down, anyway.'

Kezia is my eighteen-year-old sister who looks after me whenever Mum is busy with her laptop, mobile etc, which is nearly all the time. Mum and Dad are divorced, and Dad lives with his new family sixty miles away in Eastbury. Mum says Kezia is very responsible – I say she's bossy. Kezia's been left in charge for a few days while Mum's away on business. Mum has never left us before, and I can't *wait* for her to be back!

NO!

KEZIA (MY BEST BELOVED BIG SISTER)

Sophie looks more depressed than ever. 'I've got no money – and no life.'

'Neither have I – but look! I'm still smiling!' I give a cheesy grin, and Sophie manages a wan smile. Then, suddenly, she brightens up. I am used to her sudden changes of mood, but I am a bit taken aback by the suddenness of this one.

'YESSS!' she shrieks. 'I've got it!'

'What?' She leaps to her feet and jumps up and down on the bed beside me, so that I am being bounced too.

'An idea for making money! Lots of it! Then I could buy new clothes, and Darren would notice me. I could get my hair done in interesting colours, instead of boring blond! What colours do you think I should go for, Tash? My favourite colour is a rainbow!'

'Clothes? Or hair? *Please*, Sofe. Slow down and stop bouncing!' I grab hold of her legs, and she falls across me, giggling. 'Ouch! Get off! Right, that's better. I can do without your sock in my face, thank you. Now – explain.'

'OK.' Sophie pauses to get her breath back. 'You'd like some extra cash to splash, wouldn't you, Tash?'

'Of course I'd like some extra cash, who wouldn't? I'd like to pay Mum and Kezia back. And I could do with a new bed.'

'Right. Well, I can make your dream of a new bed come true. Here's what we do. It's what we were talking about just now that gave me the idea – I've got the gift of second sight, right?'

'If you say so.'

'Stop being such a sceptical so-and-so! It'll be OK – you'll see. I read my horoscope in *Lurve* magazine this morning, and it said – it actually said this! – that as well as my Lurve Curve being really down, money matters are bad for Gemini people at the moment.'

'Uncanny. Sorry, I didn't mean to sound sarcastic. Carry on.'

'OK. My horoscope went on to say that NOW is a good time to DO something about it. And you, being Sagittarius, which is my complementary opposite sign, as I've explained – '

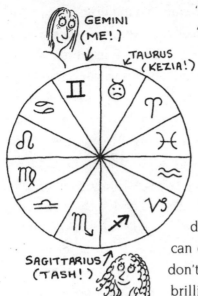

GEMINI (ME!)

TAURUS (KEZIA!)

SAGITTARIUS (TASH!)

'Many times.'

'You are the right person to do this with.'

'Do *what*?'

'Go into business together, with me doing people's horo-scopes and using my gift of second sight, if I can. The second sight thing doesn't always work, but I can do the horoscopes! Oh, don't look like that. It's a brilliant idea. It's got to succeed!'

'But you know I don't believe in all that stuff.'

'You don't need to. Just have faith in ME! I can make this work!'

'But . . .'

'No more buts.'

I lie back with my head on the pillows. So many of them, and *so* soft – I wish I had a mum like Sophie's, a mum who really cares about her children's sleeping arrangements. I could even cope with her being a bit weird and claiming to be psychic – as long as she was at home when I needed her, preparing delicious meals,

making sure the fridge was well stocked, listening to me. Sophie's mum does all of this *and* works as a librarian, in sharp contrast to my own workaholic mum . . . I close my eyes and listen to the gentle tinkling of Sophie's moon and star wind chimes, as a soft summer breeze wafts in at the open window. It is hard not to go along with Sophie when she is so full of enthusiasm. I find it infectious, although a little voice inside my head keeps repeating, 'This is a really BAD idea.'

Sophie is still enthusing. 'You'll be great at sorting out the business side, Tash – you were so quick to work out that you had minus twenty-four pounds! I'm more inspirational – a true Gemini!'

'You make me sound so boring.'

'Oh, but you're not. I didn't mean . . . sorry!'

Opening my eyes, I look at the soft reflections shining through the rainbow-coloured sun catcher in the window on to a shelf that holds an array of crystals, and some sort of weird grey rock about the size of an average brick with smooth sloping sides,

SEEING ROCK

which I don't remember seeing before.

Sophie's room certainly looks like the sort of place you'd find someone with psychic powers. The walls and nearly everything else are purple, and decorated with silver stars and signs of the zodiac. The pink net curtains billowing into the room aren't exactly to my taste, but they create the right sort of effect, like a fortune-teller's veil, and the gauzy purple and gold tasselled Chinese-style lampshade hanging from the ceiling adds to the general feel of the place. It's not my style, I'm more into the shelves-cluttered-with-make-up and clothes-strewn-across-the-floor look, but I like it because it's so . . . so Sophie. I'm just not sure about the rock.

'What *is* that?' I ask, propping myself up on one elbow and pointing at the strange grey rock.

'Ah. The rock.' Sophie looks at me very seriously, and I get the urge to giggle. 'That is my Seeing Rock.'

'Your what?'

'My Seeing Rock. You put your fingertips on it, and your energy travels through it and into my fingertips.'

'So your fingertips are on it, too – right?'

'Yes, and the rock focuses your energy into visions of things to come which I, as the Seeing One, interpret.'

'OK, now you're scaring me. How come you haven't done the Seeing Rock thing on me?' I add, trying not to feel offended.

'Because you're . . . you're too sceptical. The person I'm doing it on has to believe, or it won't work. As I've told you, psychic stuff doesn't always work – things have to be right. Anyway, you've said you don't believe in all that stuff. You don't even like my idea.'

'Oh, don't be like that! I didn't say I didn't like it! It's just that . . . well, aren't you worried that people will think we're . . . er . . . strange? I'm just . . . I'm just trying to be realistic.'

'When are you ever anything else?'

There is an awkward pause, as I feel myself teetering on the brink of a falling-out with Sophie. I don't want this, and I don't want Sophie to think I can't be inspirational, so, with an effort, I draw back, take a deep breath and say something NICE.

'It's . . . it's a great idea, Sofe.'

'Oh, I *knew* you'd like it!' Sophie exclaims, hugging me. 'I'll make it work, you'll see. And I'll give you a cut!'

'Ouch!'

'A cut of the profits, idiot!'

'Well,' I say, 'your room has the right look . . . '

'Oh, I couldn't do it in here! Mum would go majorly mad. She's told me never to use my gift on other people until I have enough experience of life to use it wisely. She says if I got it wrong, and made up stuff, I could do a lot of damage.'

'She has a point.'

'Maybe, but I'd be *careful*! And I'd only say good stuff – nothing bad, I promise.'

'So if you can't do it here, then where . . . *oh no*, Sophie! You know Kezia – she'd never allow it, so you *can't* do it at my place. The answer is a big fat NO!'

Chapter 2

Sophie

I MANAGE to get round Tash in the time-honoured way of tickling her nearly to death until she begs for mercy and says I can use her bedroom for the prediction-making business. I have a good feeling about this. I think I can make it work. I can use my gift to help people *and* make money!

The sceptical look in Tash's grey-green eyes makes me hesitate, though, and ask myself the question that occurs to me from time to time, which is: if I really *do* have the gift of Second Sight, *why* can't I see into the future *all* the time, instead of having the occasional *feeling* that something is about to happen? It happens very rarely – the last time was over a year ago, when I was at Tash's house and I had a premonition that Kezia was going to walk into the room eating a banana, and five minutes later, she did! (She *was* on a 'banana-only' diet at the time, so maybe it wasn't *that* surprising!)

A FRUIT-FLY GOES BANANAS

SHE <u>WAS</u> ON A BANANA-ONLY DIET...

I genuinely believe that Mum is psychic – she seems to be able to read *my* mind far too easily! I also think that she *wants* to believe that I have inherited it, at the same time as warning me against misusing it. (Mum and I are both Gemini, so we tend to have conflicting feelings about most things, as a result of our twin personalities.)

MUM AND I ARE BOTH GEMINI

Now Tash is asking awkward questions. She wants to know how much I am going to charge. I remind her that I am not on the business side – that's meant to be *her* thing. I am too busy searching my drawers and cupboards for a pink and gold Indian-style scarf which I can drape round my head and across my face like a veil, with only my eyes showing. Tash is wearing her usual jeans and a black strap-top which she keeps stuffed at the bottom of her school bag. I get changed into a long purple skirt with a tasselled hem and spangly silver sequins sewn on, and a floaty white blouse with lacy sleeves – *soooo* romantic! And I feel cooler now I'm out of my uniform – it's a really hot day!

'Is that what you're going to wear when you're making predictions?' Tash asks.

SOPHIE THE SOOTHSAYER

'No, it's what I'm wearing now.'

'Oh, sorry . . .'

'Just because you practically *live* in your jeans . . .'

Tash and I have different tastes in clothes – she's a real tomboy and wouldn't be seen dead in a skirt. I thought she was going to stop speaking to me when I went through my floral phase – it passed, but I still have the occasional floral moment.

THE OCCASIONAL FLORAL MOMENT...

I continue. 'So what do you think of the scarf?'

'A great improvement – I can't see you. Let me have a go.' Tash pulls the scarf off my head and drapes it over herself. 'It smells of joss sticks,' she observes, pulling it off again.

'That's a good idea!' I exclaim. 'I'll burn some when I'm doing the predictions – it'll help create the right atmosphere. Mum likes them, too – she's got loads in a drawer downstairs. Are you OK, Tash?' I've noticed that Tash always gets this sad little expression on her normally happy, friendly face whenever I mention my mum or dad. 'Do you miss your mum and dad?' I ask tentatively.

Tash shrugs. 'Mum's only gone to Nottingham for a few days, to arrange a conference for some Japanese businessmen. She'll be back at teatime on Sunday. She's visiting Gran on her way home – staying a couple of nights with her because she doesn't get to see her that often.'

'And your dad?'

'Oh . . .' Tash pauses awkwardly, 'Dad's still on at me to go and visit him.'

'You haven't been for a while.'

'No. I like being here – with you. When I'm at Dad's, I seem to spend all my time babysitting.' Tash's dad has remarried to a woman called Wendy, and they now have a baby called Alfie, who's about a year old. 'Alfie's OK,' Tash continues. 'But I feel I'm only there to look after him, and I don't even get paid! When Kezia came with me on that last visit, Dad gave her petrol money *and* some extra, I didn't get anything. It's hard to believe there's not favouritism there.'

'Maybe the extra was for food for both of you?'

'Probably,' Tash says. 'But Kezia certainly didn't give us any treats on the way home. Can we change the subject? What are you going to charge for your predictions?'

'I don't know – a pound?'

'I'd say fifty pence or twenty-five pence for half a prediction.'

This makes me giggle. I can never keep a straight face for long when Tash is around. We have this effect on each other, which sometimes means that we get sent out of lessons at school for giggling. So I might have to send her out of the room when I'm making predictions – we'll see.

Tash's next awkward question is, what am I going to call myself? She says that she needs to know for marketing purposes. She tells me that I should design a leaflet, and do some of my little drawings on it – Tash really likes my drawings – and she offers to run off some copies on her mum's photocopier and bring them into school tomorrow.

It's just as well that Dad teaches at a different school, not at St Boris's. If he found out what I was up to, he'd be bound to give the game away to Mum. They discuss everything, especially *me*! I wish they wouldn't. I always know when they're doing it, because they talk in hushed voices when they know I'm around, and, when I come into the room, they immediately stop talking and look up with unnaturally bright, cheery smiles on their faces.

We try to think of a name. 'Madame Sophie' immediately gets crossed off the list, as we both think it sounds distinctly dodgy, but we both like 'Sophie the Soothsayer'. Tash suggests that the leaflet should say, *Want to know what the future holds for* YOU? *Consult Sophie the Soothsayer! She has the answers you're looking for. Personal predictions will help you plan your life. Let Sophie put the 'scope' back into horoscope.* (We decide that this is better than

★ WANT 2 KNOW WHAT
THE FUTURE HOLDS 4
➡ U? ⬅
CONSULT
SOPHIE THE SOOTHSAYER !!!
SHE HAS THE ANSWERS YOU'RE
LOOKING 4. PERSONAL
PREDICTIONS WILL HELP U
PLAN YOUR LIFE. LET SOPHIE
PUT THE SCOPE BACK INTO
HOROSCOPPE !!!

'put the "horror" back into horoscope', which was Tash's first suggestion, and which got me giggling again.)

Then Tash says that we should include the price — *only fifty pence!* — and our real names, and where to find us at school — *third picnic table from the right of the gym at breaktime, weather permitting, to arrange a consultation to suit* YOUR *needs.*

I point out that there isn't much room left on the leaflet for my drawings, so Tash says that a border of moons and stars will be fine.

I really feel that we are getting things sorted, and that Tash is warming to my idea.

'Together we'll make this work,' I say as I get down to work, decorating the leaflet. 'We *are* complementary star signs, after all.'

I show her the drawing I have done of us as our complementary star signs.

'I like it!' says Tash. 'We look very...er...comple-
mentary. But unfortunately, Kezia *isn't* complimentary.
She's uncomplimentary.'

ME
(GEMINI —
THE TWINS)

TASH
(SAGITTARIUS —
THE ARCHER)

CLIP
CLOP

SCENE FROM SOPHIE'S SKETCHBOOK :
TASH AND I ARE COMPLEMENTARY STARSIGNS

'What star sign is she?'

'Er . . . her birthday's April 25th.'

'She's a Taurean. Don't worry, she's a pushover.'

Tash gives me a strange, you-*really*-don't-know-my-
sister look. How difficult can it be, sorting out a sister?
Kezia doesn't seem that bad to me. I have to deal with
a brother! I tell Tash that she just needs to get Kezia
trained, like I've got Kyle trained. 'The problem is,' I say,
'you and Kezia are always shouting at each other. From
what I've observed, that's not the way to go. You've just
got to work out the best way to handle her.'

No sooner are the words out of my mouth than there
is a loud *thump* on the bedroom door.

'See?' I say, trying to sound in control of the situation. 'I've trained him to knock first.' Who am I trying to fool? Tash is wearing her super-sceptical expression. 'No!' I shout. 'You can't come in!'

Kyle bursts into the room, throws himself on to my bed, and grabs the leaflet out of my hands. 'What's this?' He has short blond hair, spiked up with gel, the same blue eyes as me, but he is already a few centimetres taller than I am.

'Give it back!' I shout at him. 'It's none of your business! Eurgh – you've got mud and some sort of pond slime all over my duvet. Where on earth have you been? No, I don't want to know. Just get off my bed. And give that back!'

I make a lunge at the leaflet, but Kyle snatches it out of my reach. (I *hate* it when he does that! And he's getting taller . . . sometimes I feel as though *everyone* is taller than I am! I take after Mum – as well as inheriting her gift, I've inherited the shortness gene. And Tash is nearly a head and shoulders taller than me – she's grown a lot recently, and I *haven't* – so I'm glad she nearly always wears trainers, not shoes with heels like I do.)

Kyle is spluttering over the leaflet. 'Sophie the Soothsayer? You're joking!'

'It's not a joke!' I snap. 'And I predict that you will meet a gruesome end, being torn limb from limb by me, if you breathe a word to Mum and Dad – and I'm *not*

TASH'S TRAINERS

SOPHIE'S SHOES

joking! And I'll tell Dad that it was *you* who smashed up his marrows!' Dad is very proud of his marrows, but I caught Kyle smashing them to pieces with a stick because he hates vegetables, and Mum makes him eat them.

Kyle looks worried, and then glares at me. 'OK! OK! Keep your thong on!' He drops the leaflet.

'I beg your pardon, you rude little boy!'

'I won't tell Mum and Dad – if you keep your mouth shut about the marrows. I think you're stupid, anyway. You spend too much time in your room, reading crap magazines.'

'They're not crap! Perhaps you should read them – you might learn something.'

'I'd rather die.' And he leaves.

When I am sure he is not listening through the keyhole, as he sometimes does, I turn to Tash and say, 'There! That wasn't too difficult, was it? If I can cope with Kyle, I'm sure you can cope with Kezia.'

Chapter 3

Natasha

'WHAT ARE YOU DOING with Mum's photocopier? You know you shouldn't be touching it!'

These are the soft and gentle tones of my beloved sister, Kezia, who is standing in the doorway of Mum's study, hands on hips, staring at me with a face like thunder. Her brown eyes are glaring at me, and her wavy brown hair – not as curly as mine – is scraped back severely into a short ponytail. Some pushover!

'I'm not *touching* it, I'm *using* it. Properly. Something for school.' I just hope Kezia doesn't come over to see what I'm doing. By the time I'd finished my homework yesterday evening, I was too tired to do the photocopying, so I'm doing it now, before I leave.

'Just be careful you don't damage it, that's all! I'm responsible for the photocopier while Mum's away.'

'It's OK, Kez. You can't be responsible for *everything*.'

'Well, I *am*! Mum's left me in charge, and I have to

cope with it all, and it's not fair!'

'You don't have to be responsible for me. I can look after myself.'

But Kezia has stomped away, shouting over her shoulder at me not to be late for school. Kezia is off to Bodmington College, where she is studying for three 'A' levels, in psychology, philosophy and ethics and Spanish. She has left my lunch money on Mum's desk near the door of the study.

Folding the twenty leaflets hastily, I stuff them into my school bag, sling it over my shoulder and set off, grabbing a cereal bar as I leave. I am quite hungry, as I have had nothing since the omelette I made for myself last night – I am doing my own cooking out of an instinct for self-preservation, since Kezia's cooking poses a health threat to anyone brave or mad enough to eat it.

BREKKIE BAR
(contains nuts, raisins, oats, sawdust and chewy bits)

I don't mind walking to school when the weather's warm and dry, as it is today. St Boris's is only a fifteen-minute walk away on the outskirts of Southway, and I pass Sophie's house – 9, The Larches. I meet her there and we walk together.

This morning I decide to take a detour down the side of Sophie's house and into the back garden so that I can call up to her bedroom window. I do this occasionally, rather than endure the daily ritual of getting the front door slammed in my face by Kyle with a cry of 'Not today, thank you!' Kyle thinks he's funny – he is deluded.

'Sophie!' I yell. 'Hurry up, will you! I've done the leaflets.'

Sophie's head appears out of an upstairs window. 'Great! I'm just coming! Help! I wish I was as organised as you! I don't need to bring the rock with me, do I? I can collect it and other stuff later, and bring it to your house. We'll have to leave enough time to get ready before the first appointment, and all that . . .' Her on-the-verge-of-a-panic-attack voice trails away as she disappears into her room . . . and starts up again as she emerges out of the back door. '. . . so let's not make any appointments before four-thirty p.m. at the earliest!'

While waiting, I can't help noticing that a nearby rockery is constructed out of the same greyish rock as the one in Sophie's room.

'Do your parents know they've got a rockery made out of Seeing Rocks?' I ask as we set off about one minute later.

Sophie seems to be in a hurry to get to school, which is unusual. She apparently doesn't hear my question. 'The leaflets look great, Tash! But there aren't many of them.'

'I did twenty, and we'll be lucky if we get that many customers. Anyway, they can tell their friends . . .'

'And they can tell *their* friends . . .'

'Exactly. Word of mouth is best – and cheaper than advertising! And then you'll be famous!'

'And we'll be rich!'

As Sales Manager (appointed by Sophie, who's too scared to do it), I manage to hand out five leaflets during French without getting noticed, and another five during maths, although Mr Thornton the tall, stooping vulture-like maths teacher keeps giving me suspicious looks. By breaktime my nerves are in shreds, as the people I handed the leaflets to kept turning round during the lesson to stare at me, and one or two of the boys pulled faces and pretended to be lunatics. (I tried not to take this too personally.)

Slumping on to the bench beside Sophie (third picnic table to the right of the gym, main courtyard), I announce, firmly, 'I resign – *you* can be Sales Manager!'

'Tash! Stop stressing!'

'I'm not stressed! Look at you – you look like Stress Personified! I was just thinking, what if we don't get any customers?'

'What if we do?'

OK, this is an even more worrying prospect. W*hy* did I allow Sophie to persuade me that this was a good idea? Back in her room, surrounded by tinkling wind chimes, she made it all seem so straightforward. Now she just looks nervous, a small hunched figure with a pale oval face, trying to hide behind strands of blond hair which she is twiddling and chewing.

'Don't *do* that! I hate it when you chew your hair . . .'

Sophie's lower jaw sags.

'OK, you can close your mouth now, the hair's gone . . .'

'No, Tash! It's him – Darren. Over there!'

'Oh – yes. Can you stop clutching my arm like that? It hurts. And stop looking – you're a bit obvious.'

'I'm not looking.'

'You are – you wouldn't have seen him if you weren't looking.'

'Tash, he's coming over! He's coming over *here!*'

'Oh . . .'

Darren and his friend Scott plonk themselves down on the bench opposite us. They both have spiky light brown hair, and both are grinning. They are in Year Ten, the year above us.

'Scott found *this*, lying on the ground in the courtyard.' Darren produces one of our leaflets, badly crumpled, and smooths it out on the table in front of him. 'So – am I in the presence of Sophie the Soothsayer?' he asks.

I quickly realise that Sophie has become incapable of saying anything, sooth or otherwise. I will have to be her spokesperson.

'You are,' I reply.

'Can she speak?' Darren enquires, screwing up his

eyes and staring hard at poor Sophie, who has turned bright red. Her face clashes horribly with her maroon and yellow uniform.

'Oh, yes! Sometimes she speaks in tongues.'

Sophie darts me a horrified look and mouths, 'No!'

'Tongues?' exclaims Darren, grinning more widely than ever. 'That sounds interesting!' Scott sniggers. 'Can I make an appointment, then?'

'TONGUES'

'Er . . . yes. When?' I ask. I feel uneasy – I wish we'd never started all this, but I know that Sophie will never speak to me again if I get rid of Darren.

'Sooner the better. I want my life well and truly sorted – OK?'

'Fine, no problem. Sophie will see you at . . . at . . . four-thirty this afternoon?' (I glance at Sophie, who nods.) '. . . er . . . at . . .' (I hesitate again. I can see into the future, with me being strangled by a furious Kezia, but Sophie is gazing at me with an imploring look bordering on desperation.) 'At . . . at . . . number 10, Laburnum Way.' (I'm dead – Kezia will kill me.)

'Laburnum Way? That's near the mini-roundabout and the Joyful Shopper Minimart, isn't it?'

'You've got it.'

'See you later, then!'

Sophie gives me a sharp dig in the ribs. 'Ask him when his birthday is!'

'Oh, when's your birthday?' I call out.

'August 5th. Why? Are you going to give me a present?'

'Sophie the Soothsayer needs to know,' I shout, but he is laughing with Scott, and no longer listening.

I hear Sophie sigh. 'Leo!' she breathes. 'I just *lurve* Leo – such a noble, romantic sign, just right for Gemini.'

SCENE FROM SOPHIE'S SKETCHBOOK :

ROAR!

LEO – SUCH A NOBLE, ROMANTIC SIGN, JUST RIGHT FOR GEMINI !

Chapter 4

Sophie

OH WOW, OH WOW, oh wow, oh wow. I CAN'T BELIEVE WHAT JUST HAPPENED!!! Am I dreaming, or did Darren just make an appointment to see . . . ME!!! I ask Tash to pinch me. She does – rather hard – and tells me to stop hyperventilating. I can't help it! Darren is Lovely Leo – I can't believe it! Now I am *really* nervous. What if I still can't speak when Darren comes for his appointment? I feel such an idiot!

I ask Tash *why* she had to say that stuff about me speaking in tongues, and remind her that I find it hard enough to speak French. She just shrugs. I don't understand why she isn't more excited that we've just got our first customer – and it's Darren!!! I ask her to share in my happiness, and she just gives me this weird look. She can be a moody so-and-so, sometimes. Very Sagittarian.

'Is Kezia cool about the whole thing?' I ask.

Tash avoids meeting my eyes, and puffs out her cheeks. (I interpret this as a 'No' . . .)

'Oh . . . you . . . haven't . . . told . . . her . . .'

Tash shakes her head, and looks despondent.

'For goodness' sake! She's your sister. What's the problem? I'll talk to her – or perhaps she won't even notice what's going on.'

'Trust me – she'll notice.'

Our conversation is cut short by the arrival of another potential customer – business is beginning to boom! Tash will surely cheer up when the fifty-pence pieces start rolling in.

A tall, thin girl with shoulder-length straight brown hair and glasses is approaching us hesitantly, occasionally glancing back over her shoulder, as if worried that someone might be watching her. I recognise her as Gemma, from Tash's French group. Tash is better at French than I am, so she is in a higher group.

GEMMA

'Hi, Gemma!' says Tash. 'It's OK – we don't bite!'

'Oh!' Gemma jumps slightly, and looks nervous and embarrassed. 'It's just that I don't want Tamsin to see me. She's my friend, but she says that you're freaks, and what you're doing is stupid – and she says that I'm a freak too, if I come to see you.'

'Well! Of all the – ' I splutter. (Words fail me!)

'How dare she!' Tash exclaims. 'Are you sure you want her as a friend?'

'She's OK, really,' Gemma says, looking over her shoulder again. 'Please don't say anything to her about any of this . . . will you?'

'All consultations with Sophie the Soothsayer are totally confidential,' Tash reassures her, through slightly gritted teeth. 'Would you like to make an appointment? We could probably fit you in at five-thirty today.'

Five-thirty? That gives me an hour with Darren – is it enough? Is it too much? What am I going to say to him for a whole hour?! Perhaps he'll be late . . . perhaps he won't even bother to show up! What if . . .?

'Er, are you OK?' Gemma asks, looking at me doubtfully. 'You look totally stricken.'

'Oh, I'm fine! Don't worry, I'm just having a vision!' I smile brightly at her. 'When's your birthday?'

'September 2nd.'

GEMMA IS VIRGO

'Virgo! A born worrier. Never mind – I'm here to help. I'll sort out your personal horoscope and we'll go through it later, so stop worrying.'

'I'm not that worried.'

Tash writes her address on the back of Gemma's leaflet, just as the bell goes for the end of break.

'See you later, Gemma!' I call out. Gemma can't seem to get away quickly enough. 'There! What did I tell you, Tash? Two customers in one breaktime!'

'That's one pound, if they both show up. It's not exactly big business.' Typical Sagittarian – so impatient!

'I know, I know, but just wait till the word gets around, *then* we'll be able to splash the cash!'

I am feeling slightly less confident by the end of school. In fact, my insides are churning badly as I run most of the way home, shouting at Tash to keep up! It's another hot day, and I'm burning up.

'We've only got just over half an hour to do *everything*!' I shriek, running up the stairs to my room to get changed and grab my psychic stuff.

'Whatever is the matter?' says Mum, who has appeared in the hallway. Aargh! I had forgotten that this was Mum's day off. Mum's blue eyes are wide with surprise, as she gazes up at me questioningly. Tash is just behind her.

'Oh nothing, Mum! We've got a lot of homework, that's all. I'm going to Tash's house to do it – is that OK? We've got to time ourselves and spend just half an hour doing it. Must dash!'

Tash follows me up to my room, where I tear off my uniform (nearly strangling myself with my own tie!) and change into the purple skirt and white blouse.

'Hey, what's with all the body spray?' Tash exclaims, coughing.

'Don't want to smell of sweat when Darren gets there, do I? Plenty of joss sticks, I think – Mum let me have all these.' I stuff the joss sticks, my scarf, make-up, a load of crystals and the Seeing Rock into my bag, and hare downstairs, pursued by Tash, before bumping into Kyle and sending him flying.

'Ouch – what have you got in that bag?' he shouts. 'Rocks?'

I nearly have a fit when we get to Tash's place.

'You might have tidied up a bit!' I yell, reeling

backwards from the shock as the full, unexpurgated chaos that is Tash's room greets my eyes. It is a complete bombsite, littered with clothes, trainers, empty cans and cartons, chocolate wrappers and a plate with bits of congealed omelette on it. Her kiddies' bed is unmade, the duvet with the cute jungle creatures cover lies crumpled on the floor, and the pillows are askew.

'Are you hoping to get this exhibited at the Tate Gallery, or something?' I ask. Then I notice that Tash looks upset – sometimes I can be a bit too critical, especially when I'm stressed. 'Sorry, Tash – it was nice of you to let me use your room. Kezia's not back yet, is she?'

'No.'

'Good. Let's get ready. I'm only stressed because Darren could be here soon!'

With the curtains drawn and the lights off, and most of the rubbish shoved under the bed, the room doesn't look so bad. Tash finds some matches and we light the joss sticks and a candle. Peering into a make-up mirror

WE BORROWED KEZIA'S EARRINGS

I apply eyeliner and mascara – thickly. I hope Darren goes for the 'mystical East' look.

Tash has changed into her jeans and a navy-blue strap top. 'Wow – panda eyes!' she exclaims.

'PANDA EYES'

'Oh, now you've made me smudge it! I CAN'T DO THIS . . .'

'He's here.'

'WHAAT?!'

Tash is peering from behind a curtain. 'Get your scarf on!' she says. 'And grab your Seeing Rock. You'll be fine – pretend it's a play, like in drama at school – you're good at that. I'll go and let him in.'

'It's this way,' I hear Tash's voice at the bedroom door. 'You may now enter the presence of Sophie the Soothsayer.'

She might just as well have said, 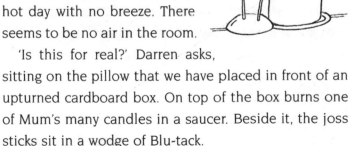 'You may now smell the presence of Sophie the Soothsayer,' as all the body spray and joss sticks in the world cannot disguise the fact that I am sweating like a pig, due to nerves and the fact that it is a hot day with no breeze. There seems to be no air in the room.

'Is this for real?' Darren asks, sitting on the pillow that we have placed in front of an upturned cardboard box. On top of the box burns one of Mum's many candles in a saucer. Beside it, the joss sticks sit in a wodge of Blu-tack.

Darren is wearing a black T-shirt with a picture of a

skull with flames bursting out of the scalp and eye-sockets – not really the sort of thing I like but it suits Darren. (Leo is a fire sign!) I am seated just behind the box on another pillow, clutching my Seeing Rock rather tightly.

I don't want Tash to go out of the room – I want her to *stay*! I am relieved when she perches on the edge of her bed. Darren is still grinning. His teeth shine rather oddly in the semi-darkness.

'Eherrrm . . .' I say, attempting to clear my throat, which feels blocked. I am *sooooo* nervous!

'Is this going to take long?' Darren asks. Tash is mouthing at me to Get On With It.

'You are Leo,' I say, in a strange, strangled voice.

'No, I'm Darren.'

'Your star sign is Leo,' I continue, my voice faltering. Tash has the giggles. 'You are honest and true. But sometimes you like to show off . . .'

'Are you dissing me?' (As if I would!!!)

'No . . .' My voice sounds weird and distant – perhaps I am about to start speaking in tongues! '. . . it's just p-part of your Leonine personality. You can't help it. And you need to be adored . . . er . . . and you *are*!'

'Really? By who?'

'I think . . . it's time for the Seeing Rock. Behold the Seeing Rock!' My hands are shaking so badly that I nearly drop it.

BEHOLD! THE SEEING ROCK!

'OK – so I'm beholding it. What now?'

'Place your fingertips upon it – that's right. What can you feel?'

'A rock.'

Tash is *not* helping – she is rocking to and fro with suppressed mirth and I have a sudden urge to laugh hysterically. I make a massive effort to control myself.

'Right, so your energy is travelling through the rock and into my fingertips. I foresee a happy future for you with a girl who loves you very, very much. I can't tell you much more except that she is Gemini, which is your complementary star sign. Oh, and your ruling planet is the Sun, so you're probably feeling pretty good at the moment because it's . . . er . . . sunny . . .'

Oh *no*. I'm going to start giggling. STOP IT, Tash! Must *not* look at her . . .

'Can I let go of the rock now?'

'Yes . . . sure . . .' (I can hear voices outside . . . Oh no! *Kezia*! I notice Tash stiffen.)

'WHO'S UP THERE?!' Kezia's voice bellows up the stairs. 'And can anyone explain why there are three boys in the front garden, grinning like idiots?'

'That would be Scotty, Jammo and Gazza,' says Darren, getting up to leave. 'I told them to meet me here. Here's your fifty pence.' He chucks it on to the box. 'Bit of a rip-off, if you ask me. And your mum doesn't seem too happy.'

'I'm Tash's sister!' snaps Kezia, marching into the room and pulling open the curtains. 'And I happen to live here! What's going on?'

'I'm out of here,' says Darren, leaving.

Oh! Don't leave! I want to call out. I hadn't finished predicting Darren's untold happiness with the Gemini girl . . . But the expression on Kezia's face is enough to stop me even thinking of calling him back.

'Explain!' she barks. 'Why has Sophie got two black eyes and a scarf round her head? And why is she wearing my earrings?! It stinks in here! Open the window wider . . .' she says, opening the curtains. 'Oh, no! It's not . . . drugs . . . is it?'

'No!' Tash shouts. 'Why do you always think the worst? It's nothing bad – Sophie and I want to earn some money, so I can pay you back, for one thing. Sofe had the idea of telling people's fortunes.'

'Well, she can't do it here! I don't want people trooping through the house and garden. Those boys were smoking, by the way. I didn't like the look of them.'

'Darren's OK,' I say. 'He goes to our school. Hey, Kezia, remind me – when's your birthday?'

Kezia looks at me suspiciously. 'Why do you want to know?'

'Just remind me.'

'April 25th. Why?'

'Ah! I thought so! You're a Taurean! You're loving and caring, gentle and kind, compassionate and understanding of others. You have the typical Taurean air of mystery, and the wonderful complexion, the beautiful hair, the warm smile . . .'

'If you think you're going to get round me . . .' But the corners of Kezia's mouth are twitching – I think it's working!

KEZIA'S A TAUREAN

'Here – put your fingertips on the Seeing Rock . . .'

'The what?'

'Just put your fingertips on this rock, and I'll tell you what I see . . . Ah! That's good! You are full of positive energy – it's flowing through the rock. You will have a happy life – oh! And a beautiful romance! A strong, caring man – probably a Scorpio – will love you forever. It's possible you might meet him near the organic fruit and veg stand in your local minimart . . .' I don't know where this last bit came from, but it sets Tash off giggling again.

'Stop! Stop! Enough!' Kezia is laughing, too. 'How do you know all this stuff?'

'I'm psychic. I've inherited the gift from my mum.' (I don't want to let on that my gift doesn't seem to be

'YOU MIGHT MEET HIM NEAR THE ORGANIC FRUIT 'N VEG STAND . . .'

working at the moment, so I'm making it up as I go along – Mum would kill me if she knew!)

'Really? So what you just told me might be true?'

'Ye–es . . .' Tash rolls her eyes – I know I can't get anything past *her*!

'Hmm . . . OK, you can carry on doing your fortune-telling, as long as it's just people from school, and not too many of them. One at a time, and no strange boys smoking in the garden, please, or you're both DEAD!'

'Oh thanks, Kezia! You're a star!' I call after her, as she leaves the room, still smiling.

I turn to give Tash the thumbs-up sign – she is staring open-mouthed, an incredulous *how*-did-you-*do*-that? look on her face.

'I told you,' I say. 'She's a pushover! It's just a matter of knowing how to handle people. Kezia's cool.'

'Gullible, you mean. I never realised she was *that* gullible! And I nearly *died* when you were saying all that stuff to Darren. You made it all

SHE'S A PUSHOVER

up, didn't you? I knew it!'

'Sometimes the Seeing Eye sees what *should* be,' I reply, stiffly. 'And you were making me laugh, which didn't help. I was seriously freaking out – you're not the only one who nearly died! I'm still shaking! Darren's fingertips and mine were practically touching.'

'Through a rock.'

'That's right. I could feel our energies bonding!'

'Oh, *puhleease*! Spare me! I didn't think much of the way he said the whole thing was a rip-off *or* the way he scarpered when Kezia arrived.'

'If Kezia hadn't disrupted the karma, I could have predicted a whole lot more for him, such as our first date! His ruling planet is the Sun, so it would probably be a hot date!'

Tash gives me her slightly pitying look, which really drives me mad. If *she* was in love, I'd be *pleased* for her – although I have to admit that she has a point about his negative Leonine behaviour . . . But any further discussion is cut short by the arrival of a nervous-looking Gemma, whom Kezia has escorted up to Tash's room.

'Don't worry! The last person who was here survived,' Kezia says, laughing as she leaves.

'Hi, Gemma. I mean, welcome to the presence of Sophie the Soothsayer!' says Tash, as I draw the curtains again. 'Please, sit down! And don't look so worried.'

'I know you can't help worrying,' I say, gently, sitting cross-legged on my pillow. 'You're a Virgo.'

'I'm really not that worried . . .'

'As a Virgo you're basically shy and possibly a bit of a loner.'

'OK, so I'm a really sad person. I didn't come here to feel worse than I already did.'

'You feel bad?'

'I often feel that really awful things are going to happen, although I don't know what – it's just a feeling. So I came here today to find out if they really are, or if I'm just imagining it.'

'I see. Yes, I SEE! That's my job! You've come to the right place. Place your fingertips on this rock.'

'Why?'

'Just do it! Please. OK – now I'm reading your energy. There's some negative stuff there . . . you must beware the crow!'

'What crow?'

'It's black . . . it flaps . . . it . . . it CAWS!'

'I *know* what a crow is. I want to know what you're on about!' Gemma's voice is high-pitched and panicky.

I have had my eyes closed. Opening them a fraction I see Tash glaring at me, mouthing the word 'No!'

'Oh . . . er . . . sorry! Got a bit carried away!' I open my eyes properly and grin at Gemma.

She does not smile back. 'I want to know about this crow,' she says, sounding scared.

'Um . . . the crow's gone. The White Bird of Joy and Happiness just chased it away.'

'You're lying. Tell me about the crow! Does it mean I'm going to die?'

'TELL ME ABOUT THE CROW!'

'No! Definitely not. Please, forget the crow!'

I *wish* I'd never mentioned it. I don't know why I did. I think there was something about the worried expression on Gemma's face that made me feel gloomy. I must cheer her up!

'I predict that you will feel a lot better soon, and a really nice boy, probably a Piscean, will ask you on a date . . .'

'It's no good – I know you're keeping something bad from me!' Gemma bursts into tears. Tash and I exchange horrified looks, and Tash leaps across the room to put her arm round Gemma.

'Hey, Gemma! You shouldn't take any of this seriously, you know. We were just mucking about! Sophie didn't mean that stuff about the crow, did you, Sofe?'

I shake my head.

'Here – have some tissues! You don't have to pay us, or anything! Just cheer up . . . please!'

Gemma manages a wan smile before she leaves. I *think* she's OK.

Tash is cross with me about the 'crow' business, and she wants to give up on the whole astrology thing. Before I go home, I manage to persuade her that I won't get carried away again, and that I'll stick to straightforward horoscopes and not bother with the Seeing Rock. I *thought* it had Special Properties – but on second thoughts, I think it might just be a rock . . .

BEWARE THE CROW!

Chapter 5

Natasha

AGAINST MY BETTER JUDGEMENT (the 'crow' business was really bad!), I am still going along with Sophie the Soothsayer! Kezia doesn't raise any objection when I run off a few more leaflets before school, although she *does* object to the untidiness of my room . . .

'I want it *tidied*, do you understand? It's a tip – a pig wouldn't want to live in there!'

She's right – any pig in its right mind would want a bigger bed . . .

'OK, Kez, I'll do it after school.' Hang on! Am I going to let her boss me around? I remember Sophie's advice not to start shouting. 'Actually,' I say calmly, in a quiet but audible voice, 'I'll do it when I feel like it.'

'You'll do it when I tell you to!' Kezia's voice is becoming shrill – that means she's not sure of herself.

In the same quiet calm voice I say, 'You can't tell me what to do.'

Kezia looks thunderstruck. She opens her mouth to say something, then seems to change her mind, and leaves for college, muttering under her breath.

'I put Kezia in her place this morning!' I tell Sophie triumphantly, as we plonk ourselves down at the third picnic bench to the right of the gym at breaktime. 'You were right – it's just a question of knowing how to handle her.'

'Sophie the Soothsayer Speaks Words of Wisdom,' says Sophie in a faraway, mystical voice.

'Hmm . . . sometimes! Gemma's not at school today, by the way.'

'Oh. Hope she's OK?'

'So do I. And where are all our new customers – they're not exactly stampeding over here, are they? And look at all those boys pointing and jeering at us. What's their problem?'

'They're not very advanced souls,' Sophie comments.

I tell the Not Very Advanced Souls to get lost – this makes them laugh and jeer even more.

'Oh, look! Here comes a customer!'

A girl called Francesca from our year approaches the picnic table.

'Hi, Fran,' Sophie calls out. 'Want to make an appointment? When's your birthday!'

'October 5th.'

'You're Libra! Luckily for you, your ruling planet of

Venus is aligned with Mars, and this could be an auspicious day.'

'Listen,' says Fran, 'I haven't come to make an appointment. Mr Banks wants to see both of you in his office – now.'

'Mr Banks?' Mr Banks is the school deputy head; a tall thin man with glasses and a moustache.

'He's read that piece about all your horoscope stuff on the news bulletin board – have you seen it yet? I don't know who wrote it.'

MR BANKS

'Oh, wow!' Sophie exclaims. 'Media coverage! That could be good for business! Why are you looking at me like that, Tash?'

I have to admire Sophie's optimism, but I have a *bad* feeling about this . . .

We have to pass the news bulletin board on our way to Mr Banks's office. Sophie, who has hurried on ahead, stops and stares at a large poster pinned to the board, on which someone has written, in block capitals: 'STEER WELL CLEAR OF THESE TWO NUTTERS!' Underneath this heading is a crude caricature of Sophie and myself with crossed eyes and goofy teeth. (I get the impression that someone doesn't like us.) It is definitely about us, since there is a copy of our leaflet pinned up, and, beside it, someone has written, in smaller capitals:

TAKE MY ADVICE – DON'T WASTE 50p
ON THESE TWO TIME-WASTERS! YOU GET
TO SIT IN A SKANKY ROOM WHILE ONE OF
THEM PRETENDS TO SEE YOUR FUTURE,
ONLY SHE CAN'T SEE WHAT AN IDIOT SHE
LOOKS. THEN THEY ASK YOU TO STROKE
THEIR PET ROCK. SAD.

'My room is *not* skanky!' I exclaim, hotly. But Sophie has tears in her eyes.

'Hey, Sofe. Don't get upset.' I rip the poster off the board, and put my arm round her shoulders. 'Just ignore it.'

'I can't – who – who would have written it?'

'Well – it can't have been Gemma.'

'So, it was . . .'

'Darren!'

I can see that Sophie is now switching into Major Crisis Mode. Her eyes are wide with shock and horror.

'Er . . . we'd better go and see Mr Banks,' I say, taking the now almost rigid Sophie by the arm and guiding her in the direction of the deputy head's office . . .

Mr Banks sits and stares intently at us, his elbows on the desk, his fingers interlocked.

'I have had a phone call from a distraught parent,' he says. 'Their daughter is refusing to attend school, or,

MR BANKS'S OFFICE

indeed, to leave the house for any reason. It would seem that she has become concerned about . . . er . . . crows. Would either of you girls know anything about this?'

Silence.

Mr Banks opens a drawer in his desk and produces one of our leaflets. 'I cannot allow you to distribute leaflets such as this at school,' he says. 'And selling your services as fortune-tellers is a very bad idea. Especially since your irresponsible activities would seem to have caused great distress to one of our students. Have you anything to say?'

'Sorry, sir. We won't do it again, sir.' Once again I

have to speak on Sophie's behalf – she is dumbstruck.

'You will spend all your morning breaktimes for the remainder of this term in detention, so that we can be sure that no further damage is done. I suggest that you apologise to the family of the student in question, and reflect upon the consequences of your ill-advised actions.'

'Yes, sir.'

Sophie comes back to my place after school. Her eyes are red with crying, and she doesn't want Kyle to see her. She is also worried that Mr Banks is going to call her parents. Her dad and Mr Banks know each other through work – they used to teach at the same school, and it would seem that they communicate on some sort of school hotline. Unfair or what?

'Mum will go mad!' she wails. 'And I *told* you it wouldn't work out between me and Darren! He's Leo – a heart-breaker.'

'Darren's a . . .' Words fail me. I pass Sophie another box of tissues – there isn't really anything I can say when she's in this sort of mood . . .

'Do you know where Gemma lives?' I ask.

'N–no . . .'

'So how are we meant to apologise?'

'I don't know.'

The answer to my question arrives at the house shortly afterwards in the form of Gemma and a man

and a woman, both wearing glasses, whom I assume are her parents. They arrive at exactly the same moment as a bewildered-looking Kezia gets back from college. We are summoned downstairs.

GEMMA AND HER PARENTS

Gemma's mum is very angry. 'She didn't want to come with me,' she says, jerking her head in her daughter's direction. 'But I made her! I want you to tell her that all this crow stuff is a load of nonsense! You're a pair of very silly girls, planting ideas like that in people's heads, especially my Gemma! She's always been sensitive.'

'Shut up, Mum!' growls Gemma. 'Sophie's psychic. She can't help seeing things in the rock – it's a Seeing Rock!'

'Er . . . hang on!' I intervene. 'That rock wasn't anything special! It was just a rock. Sophie didn't see things in it – or through it, or whatever – she was making it all up!'

Sophie looks at me with an expression on her face which is a strange mixture of hurt, embarrassment and relief, combined with obvious alarm at what I am going to say or do next. But Gemma and her parents look unconvinced – and Gemma looks as though she is going to start crying again. What can I do? Then inspiration hits me! Who says Sagittarians can't have flashes of inspiration? Not that I believe in all that stuff. 'Wait!' I exclaim. 'I've got an idea – follow me!'

Feeling like the Pied Piper of Hamelin, I find myself leading a group of people with worried and suspicious expressions out of the house, down the road and round to number 9, The Larches, where I guide them into the back garden and show them the rockery. Sophie becomes quite frantic when she realises where I am taking everyone – she keeps pulling at my arm and hissing, 'Tash! No, you can't! Mum will find out!' and 'I am SO dead.' I tell her that this is the only way.

'You see this heap of rocks?' I say to everyone, pointing at the rockery. 'Do they look familiar to you, Gemma?'

Gemma gives a slight nod.

'There is *nothing* special about them. Sophie just picked one out.'

Just then, Sophie's dad – who gets home from work about the same time as Sophie gets home from school each day – emerges from the back door. He is a thin, wiry man with receding light brown hair and round, wire-framed glasses. He looks surprised but vaguely pleased to see a group of people, led by myself and Sophie, apparently admiring his rockery.

'It is looking rather good this year, isn't it?' he says. 'I would offer to show you my prize marrows, but unfortunately I found them smashed to pieces, just the other day.'

Kyle, who has followed his dad into the garden to see what is going on, glares at his sister.

'I should think it was a badger, Dad!' says Sophie, in a loud voice.

Her dad gives a low whistle. 'Some badger! I wouldn't like to meet *that* on a dark night!'

Apart from telling me shortly that 'Horoscopes are history!' Kezia doesn't say a word as we walk home. I am feeling guilty at the memory of the resentful look Sophie threw me as we left, just as Gemma's mum and dad were just about to 'have a word' with Sophie's dad. I can't even phone Sophie on her mobile to tell her I'm sorry for making her out to be a fraud and then dropping her in it – but it seemed like the only way to convince Gemma and her parents – because Mum has put mobile call barring on our phone, and only Kezia has the pin code to take it off – and *she* won't tell me what it is! I daren't phone Sophie on her house phone. I don't want to talk to her dad or her mum.

When we get to the house – before Kezia can say anything – I turn to her and say, as calmly and quietly as I can manage, 'I think I'll go and tidy my room.'

Chapter 6

Sophie

I AM GROUNDED FOR THE indefinite future. Gemma's parents told Dad what had been going on, and Dad told Mum, who, as predicted, went majorly mad. I tried to explain that we were only trying to make some money – for some reason, this made Mum even angrier and she started ranting on about how irresponsible I was, and how morally wrong it was of me to use my gift for monetary gain, so I decided to leave it. Neither Mum nor Dad said very much about Tash, except that it was silly of her to get involved, but they were glad she'd had the sense to try and sort it out with Gemma and her parents. They don't seem to credit *me* with any sense at all!

SOPHIE'S DAD

I don't exactly *hate* Tash for dropping me in it (well – only a little bit!), and I don't really want to speak to her, although she keeps coming up to me at school and saying how sorry she is. I try not to look at her during our morning detention. I have a feeling that if I looked at her, I might start liking her again, despite myself!

I TRY NOT TO LOOK AT HER...

We sit side by side at our usual table in the canteen at lunchtime, not saying much but concentrating on our St Boris's best chicken burgers. I am taken aback when three girls from our year approach the table – I don't know them very well but I think their names are Nicole, Jasmine and Kate – and ask if I can do their horoscopes. For a moment I am tempted, but, before I can say anything, Tash has said 'no' very firmly and explained that we are no longer doing 'that sort of thing'.

I am annoyed. 'That's one pound fifty you just lost us!' I complain, when the girls have gone away.

'Don't even go there, Sofe!' says Tash. 'We're in enough trouble already.'

'But I could have done it – so easily!' I grumble. 'It's not fair! Did you see the way Nicole sort of sidled up to us sideways, like a crab? She's *got* to be Cancer! Uuurgh.' (That strange gargling noise I just made is because what happens next nearly makes me choke on my chicken burger.)

Darren comes up behind me and leans over my shoulder. 'Got any new predictions for me today, then?' he asks. 'I'm still waiting for that girl who's going to love me forever – she hasn't shown up yet, so I'm thinking of asking for my money back! Say hello to your pet rock for me – losers!' And he wanders away with Scott, laughing over-loudly and unpleasantly.

'Get lost, Darren!' Tash shouts after them. 'Oh, Sofe! Don't cry, honey!'

She puts her arm around me – we are friends again. I am so glad she is there!

FRIENDS AGAIN !

'Please, Sofe, don't cry! He's not worth it! You – you don't still fancy him, do you? Not after what he's done?'

'No! I *hate* him!' (To be more accurate, I still fancy him – but I also hate him, which reflects my twin Gemini personality.) 'I'm only crying because I'm happy!'

'Happy?'

'Yes – happy we're friends again!' This is true. 'Come home with me after school, Tash. I'll be so bored, otherwise, stuck indoors with Kyle!'

'I'd like to – but your parents probably don't want to see me.'

'They won't mind! At first they said you were silly – but then they said you were sensible . . .'

I manage to persuade a slightly reluctant Tash to come back to my house. No one is around when we get there, so we are able to slip upstairs to my room unnoticed, after raiding the kitchen for drinks, crisps, yogurts and biscuits. Tash always expresses amazement at how well stocked the fridge and the cupboards are at my house. I know that the last time Tash and I searched for something to nibble at *her* house, all we could find was a half-empty bag of prunes – and they were past their sell-by date.

'I really *am* sorry for dropping you in it, you know,' says Tash again, when we are sitting in my room, munching and listening to music – 'Fanfare for a New Age' by the Melodics.

'They would have found out, anyway,' I reply. 'A letter arrived this morning from the school, signed by Mr Banks. It said that sterner measures will have to be taken if there are any further problems. Dad wasn't too pleased.'

'Oh, great! That means there'll be a letter for Mum, too.'

There is a small knock at the door, and Tash jumps violently. Kyle puts his head round the door and smiles at us. This makes me suspicious.

'What do you want, Kyle?' I ask, sharply.

'Nothing! I just wanted to let you know that I sympathise with your plight. I know what it's like to be grounded – to be misunderstood. So keep smiling! Byee!' And he leaves.

'That was . . . nice of him,' Tash says, in a slightly doubtful tone of voice.

'That was weird,' I say. 'He's definitely up to something! He's Pisces, of course. You can never tell with Pisceans – they're a fishy lot.'

KYLE IS PISCES

Dad arrives home first, followed shortly afterwards by Mum. They are both perfectly friendly to Tash (Mum is still being tight-lipped with me!), merely saying that they hope that both of us have learned our lesson and that we won't do anything so stupid again. We promise that we won't. Mum even invites Tash to stay for tea – and Tash accepts gratefully, her eyes lighting up. She stays for tea quite often, and seems to enjoy Mum's cooking, especially the home-grown vegetables! Dad is always very pleased about this.

We help to unpack the shopping, and then I peel the potatoes while Tash prepares the carrots. (Kyle *hates* carrots – almost as much as he detests marrow!)

We go back to my room to listen to the Melodics until tea is ready. Passing Kyle's closed bedroom door, I decide to try to find out what he's up to – so I push it open . . . We discover him lying on his front on his bed, his chin propped on his hands, poring over a copy of *Lurve* magazine.

PORING OVER A COPY OF "LURVE" MAGAZINE!

'Kyle! That's my magazine!'

'Oh! Er . . . I . . .' Kyle tries to stuff the magazine under his pillow, and then realises that it is too late. He blushes bright red! I have never seen Kyle blush before!

'Why?' I ask.

'Um . . . no reason . . . I was bored.' Kyle falters. 'Thought I'd try to find out why you like these trashy mags! It's . . . er . . . quite an eye-opener! Girls have a lot to cope with. They have to read magazines like this, for a start. And it's full of pictures of other girls who look like supermodels, wearing all these skimpy clothes – it must be tough if you're not exactly . . . er . . . the right shape, because it probably makes you feel under pressure to . . . er . . . be like that!'

'My God! Kyle!' I exclaim. 'You've just had your first major insight into what it's like to be a girl. I'm impressed! But I hope that remark wasn't aimed at anyone in this room – or you're dead meat! Still, you can borrow my magazines any time, if you like.'

Kyle grins at us shyly. 'Please don't tell Tom!' Tom is Kyle's best mate – we promise not to say anything to him. 'Oh, and then I did this quiz,' Kyle continues, sounding more or less reassured, 'to find out what kind of party animal I am. And it turns out I'm a mouse, which means I'm basically a shy, introverted type who likes wearing floaty dresses and smooching to slow, romantic music.'

'OK,' I say, slowly, edging towards the door. 'Now it's getting weird. Come on, Tash – let's get out of here before he puts on a dress!'

As we leave, Kyle calls after us: 'Would you mind knocking before you come in, next time – please?'

'Oh! Er . . . yes. Sure!' I reply. I feel quite strange – I have just had a civilised conversation with my little brother.

* * *

63

Tash phones Kezia to tell her where she is, and stays on after we've had tea (sitting around the big kitchen table). Dad tells one of his excruciating jokes which Tash finds very funny, then he threatens to tell *another* joke if Kyle doesn't eat his carrots. Afterwards, we go upstairs to watch *Brompton Avenue* – our favourite soap – on the television in my room. Tash says that her mum keeps forgetting to install a television in *her* room – she must remind her.

'You and your mum are so alike!' Tash remarks. 'You've even got the same laugh!'

She's right, I suppose . . . Mum and I are both small, with blue eyes and the same straight, blond hair, although Mum's hair is cut into a shorter style.

'It must be nice, being so close to your mum,' Tash continues, thoughtfully.

'Yes – although I'm not sure that I'm her favourite person just at the moment!'

I'm so glad that Tash and I haven't allowed a failed business venture to spoil our friendship!

'Oh, but she'll forgive you! She's really kind, and understanding – like you are, when you're not stressing!'

'Er, thanks – I think. I suppose you're right about me and mum being two of a kind – we're both Gemini. Dad's Aquarius – always carrying a watering-can!'

'I'm not even sure what Mum's star sign *is*,' says Tash, a little sadly.

SOPHIE'S DAD IS AQUARIUS

'When's her birthday?'

'May 2nd.'

'She's Taurus! Like Kezia.'

'That explains a lot – they both like to make my life a misery! Like that stupid mobile call barring thing, for instance – so I can't even phone her when I want to, unless Kezia gives me permission!'

I sense that Tash is actually quite upset about the lack of closeness she feels to her mum.

'Listen,' I say, 'even if we can't make money by doing horoscopes and stuff, perhaps I could use my gift to help *you*! Oh, don't look at me like that, Tash! I *can* be helpful, you know! Even Kyle took my advice and started reading my magazines – and now he's . . .'

'Weird.'

'Right.'

'It's OK, Sofe – I know you can be helpful. You helped me get on top of the situation with Kezia. So thanks! Hey, I like those drawings!'

I have been doodling on a pad of paper on my lap – just pictures of butterflies with curly antennae and birds of paradise with flamboyant tails and magnificent crests on their heads.

'Would you do some drawings for me?' Tash asks.

I laugh. 'Here! You can have these!' I tear the page off the drawing pad and give it to her. 'Happy birthday!' I say, jokingly.

'It's not my birthday, actually.'

'So keep them for when it is. Hang on! I've had an idea!'

'Uh oh – what?'

'Greetings cards! I could make them – you could market them! It's brilliant! It's got to succeed! We can charge at *least* fifty pence for a homemade card – people love them because they've got that personal touch. We'll sell them at breaktimes – we'll be RICH!'

Tash has an uneasy 'oh-no-here-we-go-again' look on her face.

'Come on, Tash! What are you worried about?'

'Mr Banks . . . ?'

'Oh, don't worry about *him*! We'll send him a card – that'll win him over!'

'Didn't he say we weren't allowed to advertise or sell things?'

'Unless it's for charity. And it is! Our own personal charity.'

'Er . . .'

'Look, we'll even give a small percentage of the profits to the school! And there's another good thing about this, *no one* – not even Gemma – can get scared by a greetings card!'

'Just don't draw any crows . . .'

I manage to break down Tash's resistance – us Geminians can be powerfully persuasive people! She agrees to spend as much time as possible with me over the weekend – except when her mum's at home – making cards.

'I've already got masses of stuff for making and decorating pictures and cards!' I tell Tash. 'It's all in the bottom drawer of this chest over here – Mum used to buy me all this stuff to keep me busy in the holidays – I used to love doing it! Oh – this is going to be such FUN!'

Chapter 7

Natasha

I GET WOKEN EARLY (on a Saturday!!!) by Sophie texting me to find out if I'm coming over soon to help her make cards. Her mum buys her phone credit from time to time! I have a phone – Mum gave it to me last Christmas – but it never has any credit on it. I roll over and go back to sleep.

RRRING!!! The house phone startles me out of my slumbers.

'For God's sake – answer the phone!' Kezia yells from her room.

Why me? But it is too early to start an argument . . .

I stumble to the phone in Mum's room. (Mum will be back tomorrow! Then her room won't seem so empty.)

'Hello?'

'Hi, Tash!' Sophie sounds far too bright and energetic for this early hour. 'When are you coming

over? I've already made four cards – and it's only nine
o'clock!'

'I *know*.'

'I'VE ALREADY MADE FOUR CARDS!'

I find Sophie in her room with card, glue sticks, PVA
glue, bits of lace, ribbon, holographic shapes, tiny
seashells, coloured stars, sequins and glitter in all
directions. I have a look at the ones she made earlier.

'They're great, Sofe! Really . . . decorative. You've got
glitter on your nose, by the way.'

Sophie laughs. 'This is so cool!' she enthuses. 'I feel
like a little kid again, doing all this cutting and sticking
stuff. Think you could make a few?'

'I'll try . . . but we ought to do them so we can still
see your drawings. Perhaps a *little* less decoration?'

But Sophie is busy sticking tiny seashells to her next
card, and doesn't seem to hear me. 'I was wondering,'

she muses, 'do you think Mr Singh would sell our cards at the Minimart? It might be worth asking. I still want to take some to school, though. So let's get sticking!'

Listening to the wind chimes tinkling in the light summer breeze – it is another warm day, although there were clouds gathering as I walked to Sophie's house earlier – and the Melodics' CD is playing in the background, I become completely engrossed, and time passes quickly. The only interruption is when Kyle puts his head round the door and asks if either of us suffers from PMT. He's been reading magazines again.

'Get lost!' shouts Sophie, throwing a handful of seashells at him.

'Hmm,' says Kyle, retreating. 'I think you do.'

'Want to help us make cards, Kyle?' I call out.

'No, that's OK, thanks – I'll pass. I'm not really into all that "make-yourself-an-ickle-pretty-purse-or-lovely-bookmark" stuff – it's more for girls. I'm going to meet Tom.'

'He's such a boy,' Sophie comments, when Kyle has gone. 'He'll soon change his tune when you and I start raking in the money.'

After we have eaten the tuna and sweetcorn sandwiches that Sophie's mum has brought us ('Because you're so busy!' – I wonder if Sophie's mum and dad would like to adopt me??! I really like it here!),

I follow Sophie, who has a few sample cards complete with homemade envelopes in her bag, round to the Joyful Shopper Minimart. I hang back, feeling embarrassed.

'Oh, come on, Tash! Mr Singh won't mind. He won't have seen anything quite like our cards before.'

Inside the shop I find Kezia hovering near the organic fruit and veg stand, looking around cautiously and hopefully. She is wearing make-up and her tightest jeans.

'Hoping to meet the man of your dreams, Kez?' I enquire, grinning. She must have taken Sophie's prediction seriously – *how* gullible??!

'I'm just getting some broccoli!' Kezia snaps, blushing as red as an organic tomato. 'I thought I'd cook a nice meal for Mum when she gets back tomorrow.'

Uh oh, BAD idea! I don't want Mum to get food poisoning as soon as she gets back!

'Er . . . I could do it!' I volunteer, hopefully.

Kezia looks relieved. 'If you like,' she says. 'I thought we'd have a roast chicken, with roast potatoes, broccoli and all the trimmings – think you can manage that? You can ask me to help – if you get into difficulties . . .'

'Fine, no problem!'

Sophie is showing Mr Singh our cards, spread out on the counter. He peers at them closely. 'Very beautiful!' he murmurs. 'Most beautiful cards – such lovely drawings!'

Sophie and I hold our breath. 'You want me to sell these?' Mr Singh asks, staring hard at Sophie, who nods her head. 'Very well – I will have these three. I will display them here on the counter – shall we say seventy pence each? That's sixty-nine pence for you, and one penny for me!' he says, grinning.

'Oh, thank you, Mr Singh!' Sophie exclaims. 'And if you need more, we've got heaps! I can let you have as many as you like!'

'OK, OK! Three is enough! Thank you!' Mr Singh arranges the cards, and brushes a few stray sequins and tiny seashells off the counter.

Kezia inspects the cards, and looks at me enquiringly. 'It's OK, Kez!' I tell her. 'It's all above board – nothing to worry about this time!'

* * *

Kezia doesn't mind when I tell her I've been invited to stay the night at Sophie's house. Apart from a break to have supper (including a delicious rhubarb crumble made with Sophie's dad's home-grown rhubarb – Kyle seems to hate rhubarb even more than he hates carrots, so he is allowed ice cream instead),

A DELICIOUS RHUBARB CRUMBLE

and another break to watch *Accident!*, our favourite hospital drama, we work solidly on the cards until well after midnight, by which time we have made forty-seven cards. Sophie's mum found us more art materials and some more glue which she had put away 'for a rainy day'. She says that she is glad that we are keeping ourselves busy, and asks what all the cards are for. Sophie replies that they are to give to people. Some of the cards are more heavily decorated than others – so we decide to charge fifty pence for 'your basic happy birthday' which would be the plainer cards, up to a maximum of one-fifty for 'a really special card for a really special person'.

But we are too tired to write in the greetings tonight. My fingers and brain are both aching, and Sophie is noticeably less bright and cheerful than she was first thing this morning. But she is pleased with the results, and I am amazed at my own artistic achievement. I usually spend Saturday afternoons playing in the Southway All Girls (SAG) football team, but, fortunately, there is no match today – I am more into sport than Sophie is. We decide to call it a day.

'Impressive!' says Sophie next morning, surveying the results of yesterday's card-making marathon, spread out on the bed and carpet around us. We have just woken up, and it is nearly lunchtime. 'I'm starving!' Sophie exclaims. 'How about you?'

'Um, not really.' I am feeling strangely nervous and excited at the thought of Mum coming home – I just want a hug, and to feel close to her.

'Are you OK, Tash?'

'Sorry! I'm too excited about seeing Mum – I can't relax. Pretty stupid, isn't it?'

'No, it's not stupid.' Sophie seems to understand how I am feeling. 'Here – take this!' she says, rummaging in a drawer and handing me a small, smooth, pale green stone. 'It's an aventurine – the Calming Stone. Hold it in your hand when you see your mum – it'll help you relax and be happy. Don't worry, it's not like the Seeing Rock! I've tested this

THE CALMING STONE

one and it works. You can keep it.'

Although I don't really go along with all of Sophie's New Age healing stuff, I am enjoying the feel of the smooth, silky stone, cool in the palm of my hand – and it helps knowing that Sophie doesn't think I'm stupid.

'Thanks, Sofe! I'll just go and thank your mum and dad for having me to stay, and then I'm going home to be creative in the kitchen – I'm cooking a meal for Mum.'

'Oh, I love cooking! Can I help?' Sophie asks.

'Well, it would be good to have your company – but aren't you grounded?'

'Not any more – Mum and I had a chat when I went downstairs last night to get the art stuff, and she's forgiven me.'

Before I can leave, I am persuaded to stay for Sunday lunch (Sophie's friendly reassurance has brought back my appetite!), which means I'll be eating two roast meals in one day.

'How do you manage to stay so thin,' I can't help asking Sophie as we walk (or waddle – it was a BIG lunch!) back to my place, 'when your mum keeps producing all these amazing meals?'

Sophie shrugs. 'She has to use up Dad's home-grown vegetables somehow.'

Sometimes I think that Sophie and Kyle take for granted how lucky they are to have a) a dad who grows vegetables, and b) a mum who cooks them.

*   *   *

Kezia is stretched out on the sofa in the living room watching the weekend omnibus edition of *Brompton Avenue*. She *doesn't* offer to help peel potatoes, but Sophie and I are quite happy to get on with the food preparations on our own. We have just put the chicken in the oven when I hear the familiar sound of Mum's car pulling into the drive. Kezia and I rush out to greet her, and she gives each of us a big hug and says how much she's missed us, and that Gran sends her love. Everything is fine now – I don't think I need the Calming Stone any longer!

The happy homecoming is slightly marred when Kezia – bless her! – produces the letter from the school, and fills Mum in on all the details of the horoscope fiasco. Sophie looks awkward, and says how sorry she is.

'Me too!' I say, nodding.

Mum looks thoughtful. She has the same dark hair as Kezia, swept back off her pale, oval face and pinned up in a small bun – and the same brown eyes. Mine are grey-green – like Dad's. 'Horoscopes should only be for fun,' she says. 'You shouldn't take them too seriously. I hope you won't do anything like this again.'

'We won't! Promise!'

'Good – because I'm afraid I've got to go away again.'

'MUM!!!' Kezia and I chorus in despair. '*Why?*' I stuff

TASH'S MUM

TASH'S MUM IS
A TAUREAN

my hand in the pocket of my jeans where I have put the Calming Stone, and clutch it tightly.

'Oh, please don't be upset,' says Mum, looking almost as distressed as we are. 'I feel bad enough about leaving you again, but we really could do with the money I'll be earning, if I do this . . . I have to arrange a huge conference in Runchester. I'm not going till Wednesday. I'll be gone for four days – that's all! You *do* understand, don't you?'

'Will you be able to afford to buy me a new bed?' I blurt out, angrily (I feel hurt – she's leaving me again).

'Oh – of course, darling! I'm so sorry – I MUST get round to it.'

'Do you think I'd better leave?' Sophie whispers to me, as she and I go out to the kitchen to check on the supper. She has been silent until now, looking awkward – I feel suddenly guilty.

'No! Stay, please – I'd like you to! You can phone

home, if you like, and let them know.'

Mum goes upstairs to unpack and have a bath. When she comes down again she looks refreshed, and gives us some little soaps, shampoos and conditioners that she sneaked into her luggage from the hotel where she was staying.

Supper is delicious (but I seem to have lost my appetite – again) and Mum asks us how we're getting on at school and college. I ask how Gran is – I wish I could see her. Mum replies that Gran is well, and about to go and visit a friend in Scotland. We are all being very polite. This is an effort – I want to shout at Mum that I don't want her to go! I want her to stay home and make delicious meals with home-grown vegetables – but more than that, I just want her to Be There.

'If you like, I could arrange for you to go and stay with Dad next weekend,' Mum suggests. 'While I'm away?'

'Er – no. That's OK,' I reply, awkwardly. 'He's already

phoned twice while you've been away, wanting me and Kez to go and stay for a weekend. But I said I was busy – I've got a lot of . . . er . . . homework. I don't think he was very pleased.'

'OK – well . . . if you're sure . . . But if it was for longer than four days, you'd have to go . . . Oh, please cheer up! Shall I help you stack the dishwasher?'

'Come on, Tash!' says Sophie. We are standing in the hallway, and she is about to go home. 'Don't look so sad! You know where I am if you need me, and you've got your Calming Stone – you'll be fine! Aren't you pleased that your mum is home?'

'Yes, I *am* pleased! But she's going *again*!'

'Not for long – and not till Wednesday. Anyway, you and Kez can have wild parties! I'd give anything to have my parents out of the way. And – hey! – I'*m* not going anywhere! Remember me? Your best mate?!'

I can't help smiling. 'Thanks, Sofe – you always cheer me up. But I'm not sure I'll get away with the wild parties, not with Kezia around.'

Sophie laughs, and gives me a hug. 'Now,' she says, holding on to my shoulders and looking into my eyes, 'I want you to start focusing on what's happening tomorrow – our latest and greatest scheme for becoming very, very RICH! Do you think we need to bring all the cards into school tomorrow?'

'Er . . . no. I think about ten or so might be enough . . .'

'OK, we'll build up the business gradually. So we'll charge fifty pence for your basic birthday card, up to a maximum of one pound fifty for a Very Special One . . . And we'll only show them to people who are likely to be interested.'

'Not Darren.'

'No, not Darren.'

I am about to go to bed. I have placed my Calming Stone under my pillow in the hope that it might transfer its calming influence to my stressed mind while I sleep – not that I really believe it *will*. The phone rings.

'It's for you, darling,' Mum calls upstairs to me. I've just spent an evening sitting with Mum on the sofa – nice – except that she spent her whole time rattling away at the keys of her laptop and making or taking calls on her mobile – AS USUAL! You'd *think* that she could have spared me a few moments of undivided attention! But no. 'Take it in my room, if you like – it's Sophie,' Mum calls.

Perching on the edge of Mum's double bed, I pick up the receiver and hear Sophie's voice, sounding panicky. 'We haven't done the greetings!'

'Greetings?' I am tired – my brain isn't working properly.

'Yes! They're meant to be *greetings* cards, remember? But we haven't written in any greetings – so they're just cards!'

'OK, so write some greetings in them. What's the big deal? Or they can be blank cards – you write in your own greeting.'

'No! I want them to be special! With verse, or something.'

'No,' I say, firmly, '*not* verse! Come on, Sofe – I'm sure you can think of something. I'm really tired – I've GOT to get to bed.' I wish Sophie wouldn't get so stressed by trivial things – I'm the one with *real* problems.

Chapter 8

Sophie

'GREETINGS!' TASH CALLS OUT.

I am waiting for her outside my house, ten of our beautiful cards carefully placed in the zipped front compartment of my school bag, where I usually stuff my games kit.

'Don't talk to me about greetings,' I retort. 'I was up until one o'clock in the morning doing those! Hey, great news! I told Mum about your mum going away again, and she said you can come and stay with us, if you want to.'

'Oh, wow! Oh . . .' Tash hesitates. 'I really *want* to stay with you. But what about Kezia? I can't leave her all on her own – she can't even cook! And she had the cheek to complain to Mum over breakfast, which Mum cooked – which is unheard of, so I think she must be on some sort of guilt trip. Anyway, Kezia had the cheek to complain about how unfair it was, leaving her with the responsibility of looking after *me*!!! And they were talking like I wasn't even there, in the room, listening.'

'Right.' I understand how Tash feels, but I don't always know what to say – at least she doesn't have to live with a not-so-little brother whose idea of a joke is to put a live frog in my school shoe! I am still shuddering from the soft, slimy sensation which greeted my left foot this morning – fortunately, for the frog, I didn't squash it.

'Oh, but I really *really* want to stay with you!' moans Tash, who is obviously struggling with the dilemma of whether or not to leave Kezia on her own.

'I think you should,' I say, firmly. 'Can't Kezia have a friend to stay, or something? Anyway, a few days living with Kyle and you'll appreciate how lucky you are to live in an all-female household! Don't worry about Kezia – we can visit her every day, and take her food parcels.'

* * *

Breaktime – and Tash and I are back at the third picnic table to the right of the gym, each of us clutching a handful of greetings cards, uncertain who to approach first.

'Oh, look!' I say to Tash. 'There's Gemma! I'm glad she's back. Perhaps she'd like to buy a card. Hey, Gemma! Want to see some cards?'

Gemma backs away, looking horrified. 'Tarot cards?' she says, hoarsely.

'No! Greetings cards! Nice, pretty ones, with decorations – look!'

'Er, no thanks!' says Gemma, and she turns her back on us and walks away.

'What's *her* problem?' Tash exclaims, hotly. 'Anyone would think we were going to attack her!'

Our cards attract a small crowd of girls, who seem to like them.

'I want one for my mum,' says a short round girl with bouncy reddish-brown curls and freckles. 'But I'll have to bring the money in tomorrow.'

'That's OK – you can owe us,' I tell her, handing over the card.

By the time the bell goes for the end of break, Tash and I are feeling very pleased. We have sold a total of six cards: two of the plainer ones at fifty pence each, three of the more densely decorated ones at seventy pence, and a boy called Jason bought a 'Very Special' one for his girlfriend for one-fifty, which he has promised to bring to school tomorrow. The greetings card business seems to be taking off, and I am so elated that I don't even get upset when Darren sneers at me and Tash, and shouts, 'Rip-off!'

My elation is short-lived. During a history class with Miss Roberts, I am aware of a lot of whispering and giggling going on around me – and several people dart glances in my and Tash's direction. It is obvious that something is being passed around which is causing great amusement, and I think I can guess what it is.

'Hand it over!' says Miss Roberts, wearily. 'Whatever it is.'

One of our cards is passed to the front of the class, and Miss Roberts opens it, frowns, and then reads aloud:

'You make my heart
Go ding dong ding
So how about it
Let's have a fling!'

The class collapses. Tash is glaring at me furiously – but before either she or Miss Roberts has a chance to say anything, the door opens and a boy comes in and says, 'Please, Miss – Mr Banks wants to see Natasha Phillips and Sophie Edwards in his office – now.'

* * *

'I *told* you not to do verse!' Tash hisses at me as we make our way to Mr Banks's office. 'I should have checked all the cards – I might have known you'd go and do something stupid!'

'You're blaming *me*? *You* didn't exactly offer to *help* do the greetings, did you? It was late, and I was tired . . .'

'That's no excuse for bad verse. Anyway, hearts don't go "ding dong ding!" – at least, mine doesn't.'

My heart is going 'thump thump thump' as we stand in front of Mr Banks's desk, and he regards us over his interlocked fingers. I have a sense of déjà vu.

'It would seem that you haven't got the message,' he says. 'I cannot allow the school premises to be used for commercial dealings intended to line pupils' pockets, and I understand that you have been selling cards.'

'We could make a contribution to the school funds!' I suggest, hopefully.

'I'm sorry, that is not the point. You didn't have permission, and your cards have been the cause of disruption in some classes. Mr Horrocks confiscated this . . .' He produces a card which we sold to a girl in Kyle's year. '. . . during biology. A group of students were laughing at it instead of concentrating on their work – they were given detentions. And I hardly think it's suitable, do you?' Mr Banks opens the card and reads aloud:

'Forget about your education!
And listen to my explanation!
You and me – we're the next sensation
Like Adam and Eve and the Creation.'

'Well?' he says. 'What do you have to say for yourselves?'

'It's rap, sir,' I explain, shifting uncomfortably, and aware that Tash is staring at me with an expression of mingled incredulity and disbelief on her face. 'It's like rap music, only it's . . . er . . . poetry.' It seemed like a good idea at the time, when inspiration struck me, just after midnight alone in my room. But now, here in Mr Banks's office, it doesn't seem as good.

'Poetry, eh?' Mr Banks muses. 'Unfortunately, despite the fact that the drawings on the front of the card are delightful, and you have . . . er . . . gone to a great deal of trouble with the decoration, I cannot at all approve of your advice to students to "forget their education". And if you'd read the Bible properly, you may recall that Adam and Eve came to a sticky end, and God cast them out.'

Oh no! Is he going to exclude us? Mum and Dad will *kill* me!!!

'Your parents will have to be informed, and I'm afraid that you will both lose your lunchtime breaks as well as morning ones for a week. In the meantime, I want all cards to be removed from the school premises, and *no* further incidents, do you understand?'

'Yes, sir!'

'Good. And I don't want to see you again.'

'I am *so* dead!' I moan, as we make our way back to lessons, just as the bell goes. 'Mum and Dad are going to freak.'

Before Tash can say anything, the boy called Jason who bought the Very Special card marches up to us and exclaims, 'I'm *not* paying you *anything* for *this*!' He produces a slightly creased card from his bag – it has lost most of its decorations – it had an under-the-sea theme – and there are just a few shells sticking to it, and a stray ribbon, along with splodges of dried glue. 'Look!' he shouts, angrily. 'It's *moulting*!' And he throws it down at our feet in disgust, and marches off.

'But you can still see the drawings!' Tash calls after him. 'And they're fantastic!'

'Thanks, Tash!' I say. I feel embarrassed, but it's good of her to stand up for me, especially after I have just landed her right in it with Mr Banks. 'But I guess we should have used stronger glue. Although it wasn't *our* fault if he just stuffed it in his stupid bag, and didn't take proper care of it.'

By the time we get out of school at the end of the day, we have been shouted at by another angry customer –

a boy who got a detention in biology because his friends were laughing at his card. He demands his money back as compensation, and we give it to him, just to get rid of him. He tells us that his friends want to sue us, because *they* got detentions, too. Tash has stopped standing up for me – now she looks tired and fed up . . .

'*That* was a complete disaster,' she remarks, as we make our way home. 'And a complete waste of time, making all those cards! We went to such a lot of trouble, too – although I wish you'd taken my advice and cut down on the amount of decoration – and *why* oh *why* did you have to do VERSE – I TOLD you not to!'

'OK! Stop saying "I told you so!"' I protest. Tash manages to make it sound as though it is all MY fault! 'Anyway, we had four customers who *didn't* want their money back.'

'And three of them *owe* us the money.'

'So? I've got fifty pence here – I'll split it with you – and we've still got our outlet at the Minimart, even if we can't sell cards at school!'

Tash gives me a withering look. 'I think I'll just go home,' she says.

'Oh no you *don't*! You are *not* leaving me to face Mum and Dad on my own – like you did the last time!'

'But they're *your* parents!'

'Yes, and they're pretty nice to you! You're invited to stay – remember?'

'Don't know if I want to!'

'Well *don't*, then!'

'OK, I *won't*!'

'Fine!'

'*Fine by me*!' Tash retaliates. 'Oh, by the way – your Calming Stone DOESN'T WORK!!!'

And she storms off.

'Tash!' I call imploringly, but not loud enough for her to hear. I really don't want to fall out with her, but I don't feel like apologising. I am too confused and upset by what just happened to think straight.

To make matters worse, Dad is waiting for me when I get home, and he doesn't look happy.

'I had a phone call from Gordon Banks,' he informs me. Oh, great! 'What *are* you playing at?' Dad demands, angrily. 'This has got to *stop*!'

'It will, Dad. It already has,' I say, sadly. I don't care about the cards any more – I don't want another failed business venture to come between me and Tash.

Mum doesn't freak quite as badly as I had feared. She seems more concerned to know *why* I have been doing these things, and she quickly realises that I am feeling sad – I am so glad that she understands me! When she's in a listening mood, I find it very easy to talk to her. So I tell her how Tash and I wanted to earn some extra money, but it all went wrong – and now Tash isn't talking to me, and I'm worried that she blames me for everything. With a pang of guilt I explain that Tash tried to talk me out of it – both times.

Mum looks thoughtful. 'I wish you'd talked to me first,' she says. 'If it's just a matter of earning extra pocket money, Dad and I can give you some jobs to do. Hang on!' she says, beaming at me. 'I've had an idea!' Mum and I are similar in many ways – inspiration tends to strike us suddenly.

'What?'

Mum tells me that she has a friend, Babs Ames, who has a large house and garden at 4, Sycamore Way (a road lined with smart houses, not too far away). Mum's friend is about to go to Australia for a month to do research into small, furry marsupials for a book she is writing, and she is looking for a reliable, trustworthy and responsible person whom she would pay to come in and water her plants, do the dusting, mow the grass and

RESEARCH INTO SMALL FURRY MARSUPIALS

generally keep an eye on the place while she is away. She has been let down by the person who was going to do the job, and now she is panicking, as she is due to leave this Thursday . . .

'Tash and I could do that job!' I exclaim. 'We can be responsible! And it'll be even easier, if Tash is staying with us . . .' My voice trails away.

'Yes,' says Mum. 'That's probably true. But there's a bit more to it than that.'

Mum explains that her friend's house has a granny annexe, where her elderly mother lives. 'You'd be expected to keep an eye on Mrs Clarkson – she's Mrs Ames's mother,' says Mum. 'She's very independent, and good for her age – she's eighty-six – but she can't walk very far. You'd have to do her shopping, if she needs any, as well as giving her a bit of company.'

'We can do that! No problem.'

'And then there's the dog.'

'Dog?'

'Yes, Crumpet the dog. Babs dotes on him, but she can't take him to Australia.'

'Because he'd chase the small, furry marsupials?'

'Something like that!' Mum laughs. 'And she doesn't want to put him in kennels, because last time she did that, he nearly died of kennel cough. Her mother can look after him during the day, but she can't take him for walks. I think Babs was hoping that I'd do it all, and look after granny and the dog – but I'll try and convince her that I've got a *very* responsible daughter.'

'And Tash!' All of this will surely help me make it up with Tash – I hope!

'Yes, I won't forget about Tash. You'd have to go in before school, and let Crumpet out for a run round the garden, and then go back after school to take him for a walk, and do everything else. It's quite a lot – I don't want it to interfere with your schoolwork.'

'Oh, it won't, Mum. Promise!' I really want to do this job – I love dogs! And grannies – especially since two of my own grandparents – Dad's parents – are no longer alive, and I hardly ever get to see Mum's parents, who live in Spain.

Mum gives me a hug. 'Leave it with me!' she says. 'I'll see what I can do.'

Chapter 9

Natasha

I AM WOKEN BY ANOTHER TEXT message from Sophie. She kept sending them after we fell out yesterday, but Mum was on the phone to her colleagues nearly the *whole* evening, and by the time she'd finished, it was too late to call Sophie's house, and I *still* don't have any credit on *my* phone! The latest message from Sophie, like all the others, carries an apology:

'GREETINGS – SORRY! I REALLY AM SORRY! PLEEEASE CAN WE BE FRIENDS? DON'T U WANT 2 KNOW WHAT MY NEWS IS? C U SOON! WALK 2 SCHOOL WIV ME? LOL. XXXXXXX.'

Sophie is mad, but I like the way she never bears a grudge – I *do* want to make it up with her and I *do* want to go and stay. I wonder what her 'news' is? Not another money-making scheme, I hope! What's it going to be this time – making cakes and biscuits? Or something more adventurous, such as organising hang-gliding holidays for hamsters? Nothing would surprise me.

A grim silence greets me in the kitchen. Mum is sitting at the table, drinking a cup of black coffee. Her guilt trip seems to have come to an end, and she hasn't cooked anything this morning.

'Hi, Mum! Is everything OK?'

'No, Natasha, it isn't. I've had another letter of complaint about your behaviour from school. It says that they tried to phone here yesterday, but there was no reply – that must have been when I was at the hairdresser's. But I really think I have enough to cope with without these letters – AND I DON'T WANT ANY MORE, DO YOU UNDERSTAND!?!'

I nearly jump out of my skin – I hate it when she shouts. She continues: 'IF THERE'S ANY MORE TROUBLE, YOU'LL HAVE TO GO AND LIVE WITH YOUR DAD!'

'I don't care!' I shout back, feeling my face flush and hot tears rush into my eyes – does Mum really think that the only way to get through to me is to yell at me and remind me (as if I need reminding) that she and Dad are no longer together? And I *do* care – I love Mum, even though she's being horrible, and I love Dad – but I wish he didn't live so far away, as I don't want to leave all my friends, especially Sophie. I turn and head out through the kitchen doorway.

'Where are you going?' Mum shouts after me. 'You haven't had any breakfast.'

'I don't want any!'

I storm into the living-room to collect my bag, which I've left on a chair, and find Kezia, reading her horoscope in the newspaper.

'Too much shouting, too early in the morning,' she comments, without looking up. 'It says here that your ruling planet of Jupiter is no longer aligned with Mars, and you may experience conflict.'

'I don't have time for this!' I snap. 'Why aren't you going to college?'

'Oh, I'm taking the day off so Mum and I can go shopping together at the mall before she has to go away again. It was her idea – you can't come because you have to go to school.'

I stare at Kezia mutely. I am having my Final Straw Moment. It is a few seconds before I can speak . . .

'Right!' I say, stiffly. 'I'm going away too – tomorrow.'

'Oh?' Kezia looks up from her newspaper. 'Where?'

FINAL STRAW MOMENT

'I'm going to stay with Sofc while Mum's away – I've been invited.'

'Does Mum know?'

'No. I'll tell her – later.'

'OK.' Kezia resumes her reading of the horoscope page. 'Do you . . . er . . . mind?'

'No, why should I?'

'You might . . . er . . . miss me! Or be lonely – you could have a friend to stay . . .'

'Well, you're only going to be down the road and round the corner, aren't you? It's not as if you're going to Australia. Don't be so daft!'

Sophie is looking anxious by the time I get to her house – she is waiting outside for me. A few raindrops are falling.

'I thought you weren't coming!' she says.

'Well, I *have* to come this way, don't I?'

We look at each other seriously for a few moments, then I shout, 'Oh, for goodness' sake!' and we give each other a Big Hug. Sophie is laughing and crying at the same time – talk about a typical Gemini! (If you believe all that stuff.)

'Did you get my messages?' Sophie asks. 'Shall I tell you the news?' I can see that she is bursting to tell me!

'Go on . . .'

'Well, and you don't need to worry this time because it's not even my idea – it's Mum's! So it'll be fine.'

'Sophie! Just tell me!'

'OK.' Sophie tells me all about Mrs Ames and the house and the garden and the granny and the dog.

'Sounds great, Sofe!'

'So you *are* coming to stay, aren't you?'

I tell Sophie that wild hippopotamuses couldn't stop me, and her eyes shine with happiness. I am feeling so much better now – having a friend like Sophie makes everything else seem bearable.

'Mum's going to talk to your mum,' says Sophie, 'just to make sure that she's cool about you coming to stay, and doing that job for Mrs Ames – her name's Babs, by the way – and everything. But they've always got on well, haven't they – our mums? So there shouldn't be a problem.'

'Mum won't mind,' I say. 'She couldn't care less.'

Sophie gives me a searching look. 'How are things between you and your mum?' she asks.

'Since you ask – *bad*,' I reply. 'I don't think I want to talk about it. I'm just looking forward to coming to stay with you and your family.' A nice, warm, friendly, *normal* family – as opposed to mine.

'OK – well, if you ever feel you want to talk about things.'

'Thanks, Sofe.'

'By the way, Mum says Kezia can come to stay, too, if she's lonely – we've got room.'

'Oh! Er – I think Kezia's happy staying where she is, but I'll tell her. Thanks!'

It's not been a wonderful day. I stormed out of the house this morning without my lunch money (so was deprived of my usual chicken burger). I spent morning and lunchtime breaks in detention, and the rest of the time avoiding people whose cards have been moulting; the people who still owe us money are refusing to pay. Then I got soaked by a sudden downpour as I walked home.

I don't think I can cope with any more conflict, and I wish that my ruling planet would realign itself with Mars. But Mum is being nice. She has even bought me the light blue strap-top I wanted (Kezia smiles at me, and says that she told Mum about it, and showed her where it was), some body spray, and a tub of my favourite intensive hair conditioner. Another guilt trip? I'll bet she regrets yelling at me this morning!

'Oh, thanks, Mum! And thanks, Kezia!' While Mum goes out to the kitchen to attend to the supper, I tell Kezia about Sophie's mum's invitation to her to go and stay – Kezia says thanks, but that she's happy to stay at home.

After a long hot bath, relaxing in the perfumed water (Watermelon Magic Bath Fragrance), drinking a mug of steaming hot chocolate and eating Bourbon biscuits (I like to do this in the bath – when Kezia has remembered to buy Bourbon biscuits), I come downstairs wearing my new strap-top, my favourite jeans (which Mum has washed and ironed!), with my hair intensively conditioned – and I realise that I don't want Mum to go, and I am going to miss her. I tell her how I'm feeling. She gives me a big hug, and tells me that she's going to miss me too, but that it won't be forever. Then she says that she's sorry for being so cross this morning, but that it was a shock getting another letter from the school – I promise her that it won't happen again. She gives me a ten-pound note to buy phone credit. My ruling planet has obviously realigned itself in some style!

As we tuck into Mum's special shepherd's pie (my favourite – I think Mum knows that!), Mum tells me that she had a phone call from Sophie's mum, and that she's happy for me to go and stay with Sophie and her family. She will leave me with enough lunch money to cover the next few days ahead. She also says that she thinks that the work for Mrs Ames sounds like a good idea, especially with Sophie's mum nearby, to keep an eye on the situation and lend us a hand, if we need help.

'Perhaps one of you two girls' – Mum looks at me and Kezia – 'would like to cut *our* grass – it's a wilderness out there!' This is true – I remember when Dad used to cut the grass. Mum has never really got into the habit of doing it herself, so Kezia or I usually do it.

'IT'S A WILDERNESS OUT THERE!'

'Don't look so sad, darling!' Mum says to me. 'I think you're going to have a great time!'

Chapter 10

Sophie

TASH WAS IN TEARS WHEN she arrived in a rain shower at my house this morning to go to school. I asked her if it was because things were bad between her and her mum. She said, No, it was because things were so good, and she didn't want her mum to leave – and she's just gone. (I find Tash's relationship with her mum confusing – but I'm glad things are better than they were.)

Tash cheers up as the day goes on – despite the detentions – and it stops raining and the sun comes out. After school we collect her stuff from her house and bring it to mine. Tash has a *lot* of stuff. She tips it out of her bag all over my bedroom floor, which gives my room a slightly different look; I prefer to fold my clothes, and put them away neatly – but I don't want to upset Tash by complaining as soon as she gets here. I clear some crystals off a shelf, and tell her that she can put her body sprays, cleansing pads, intensive hair

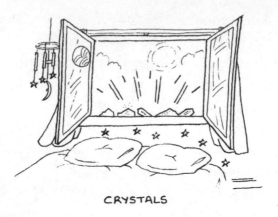

CRYSTALS

conditioner etc. up there. I put the crystals on the window sill, where the warm sunlight will recharge their natural healing properties. The sky has cleared, and the day is now quite hot and steamy.

Kyle sticks his head round the door, and says, 'Oh no, not *two* girls – one was bad enough! Now I'm going to have to cope with *two* lots of pre-menstrual tension.'

I throw one of my magazines at him, and he leaves, shouting, 'I've already read that one!'

Tash and I go down to the kitchen to get a drink and a snack, and agree that we will never let *anything* come between us again.

Mum tells us that Mrs Ames has agreed to let us do the work! She will pay us *each* a hundred pounds when she gets back from her trip. My jaw drops. Tash gives a low whistle.

'A hundred pounds!' I exclaim. I'll be able to shop till I drop! Not that I'll be buying clothes to impress Darren, like I'd planned – I don't think there's much point, so I'll be getting them to cheer myself up! 'The mall – here I come!'

'And I'll *nearly* be able to afford that double bed I saw in my mum's catalogue!' Tash says, enthusiastically. 'I showed it to Mum – she liked it.'

Then Mum tells us that we've been invited to go round to Mrs Ames's house this afternoon to meet her mother, and Crumpet the dog, and be shown where everything is – so we'd better hurry up! Mum is coming with us, as Mrs Ames wants to give her a set of house keys – 'just in case' – and make sure that everyone understands what they are expected to do before she goes tomorrow!

Mrs Ames's house in Sycamore Way is a very grand red-brick building with a wide front lawn (it doesn't need cutting – yet), and a straight gravel path lined with lavender bushes. The path leads to a short flight of stone steps up to the front porch, which is supported by Greek-style columns. When Mum presses the doorbell we hear excited barking.

'That must be Crumpet!' I exclaim.

The words are hardly out of my mouth when the door opens, and a flurry of golden fur hurtles out, skids on the steps and starts jumping up, trying to lick everyone at once.

'Crumpet! Down!' roars a large bouffant-haired lady in a tent-like floral dress. This must be Babs (not the frail old lady!).

'BABS'

'Come in! Come in!' barks Mrs Ames. 'Be *quiet*, Crumpet! DOWN, boy! I'm so sorry – he's still quite young – boundless energy! SIT!!!' (The small, furry marsupials are going to be scared out of their wits by Babs.)

The golden retriever sits, panting, his bottom wiggling and his curly tail sweeping from side to side. He gazes at us appealingly out of melting brown eyes.

'Oh, he's beautiful!' Tash and I crouch down to stroke him, and he licks our faces.

'He's certainly a handful!' booms Mrs Ames. 'Come and meet my mother – she's in the annexe. *Heel*, Crumpet!' The granny annexe is a light, airy extension built on to the back of the house, with its own kitchen, bathroom, bedroom and living area. A tiny, frail old lady with wispy white hair – she looks as though she's just

CRUMPET

been out in a high wind – is sitting in a chair, slightly turned away from us, watching television. She turns and smiles at us. She is nothing like her daughter!

'Mother!' booms Mrs Ames. 'This is Mrs Edwards, her daughter Sophie and her daughter's friend . . . er . . .'

'Tash.'

'Tash! These are the two young girls who are going to look after everything while I'm away. Their mother will be close at hand to supervise – I'm leaving her phone number with you. . . '

Elderly Mrs Clarkson beams at us. 'So nice to meet you! I'm afraid I'm a little deaf – were your names Susie and Taz? I've met Mrs Edwards before, I'm sure I have. Please – sit down – help yourselves to biscuits.' There is a plate of Bourbons on a little table beside the elderly lady's chair.

'Thanks!' says Tash, helping herself. 'I'm Tash! It rhymes with cash!'

Mrs Clarkson beams, and adjusts her hearing aid. Babs brings the tea, having taken Tash and me on a lightning tour of the main part of the house, showing us where the Hoover, cleaning materials, tea-making equipment etc. are stored and where all the plants are, especially the ones in pots. 'Don't forget to water them, but don't *overwater* them – and please water the outdoor pots every day if it doesn't rain!' She also shows us where the phone is situated. 'For emergency calls *only*!' she barks. We nod and then go to say goodbye to Mrs Clarkson, until tomorrow after school, which is when we are required to make our first visit.

Babs takes us into the back garden, which has a huge lawn, sloping gently downhill to a screen of fir trees at the far end. The lawn is bordered by flowerbeds, bursting with vivid colours, and we are shown where the lawnmower, hose and other gardening implements are kept. Crumpet is going berserk careering madly up and down the garden, ears flapping, barking his head off.

'Crumpet! You mad thing!' exclaims a young man's voice.

Tash and I turn our heads in the direction of the voice at exactly the same moment; a sun-bronzed, bleach-haired boy of about seventeen – BARE-CHESTED!!! – is looking over the hedge at us from the house next door's garden. I t*hink* he is looking at me, rather than at Tash – or he may just be looking at Crumpet, who rushes up to the hedge and starts jumping up at him frantically.

'Hello!' he calls to us, over the barking. 'I'm Gareth. Who are you?'

'I'm Sophie.'

'I'm Tash.'

GARETH — THE 'SUN GOD'

Gareth grins a little shyly, and reaches down to pat Crumpet, his strong, brown arms shiny in the late afternoon sun with what must be suntan oil, his tanned skin contrasting with his short, spiky bleached hair. (Oh – WOW! My Lurve Curve has just done a loop-the-loop! I couldn't care less about Darren any more – he is a thing of the past! My future is with Gareth the Sun God! I wonder if he has a girlfriend?

'Hello, Sophie and Tash – and Crumpet!' he says.

'Hi, Gareth,' says Tash in a sort of girly, flirtatious tone of voice which I do not normally associate with her. It doesn't suit her. 'We're going to be working here, while

Mrs Ames is away, so you'll probably be seeing us again – at least, I hope so!'

Oh my god, how *obvious* can you get? It's *embarrassing*! I'm sure that Gareth is the sort of boy who will go for my more subtle approach.

'Hi, Gareth,' I say, in a non-flirtatious but gently encouraging tone of voice. 'Beautiful weather, isn't it? You've got the right idea – sunbathing! I can't *wait* to get into my bikini!'

(Tash is giving me one of her looks – what's her problem?!)

'I was going to do your job,' says Gareth, nonchalantly. (Maybe he didn't hear what I just said. I was hoping for some kind of reaction.) 'But Mum said I ought to concentrate on my studies – I'm a bit behind – and I'm already working three evenings a week at Pizza Palace.'

'I like pizza!' Tash exclaims.

(Shut up, Tash – now it is my turn to give *her* a look!) 'What are you studying?' I ask.

'I'm at sixth-form college in Bodmington – studying for A-level maths, physics and chemistry.'

'My sister goes there,' Tash says. 'But she's doing different subjects.'

WE BEHOLD THE SUN GOD

'What's her name?'

'Kezia.'

'Kezia . . . No, I don't think I know her.'

Our conversation is interrupted by Babs, who has been trying to attract our attention. 'Girls!' she bellows. 'No flirting with the boy next door – beautiful as you are, Gareth – allowed while you're working here, I'm afraid!' She guffaws loudly.

Tash and I freeze – I am going hot and cold all over, and Tash has gone bright red. Gareth disappears.

'Do you think Gareth will ever talk to us again?' Tash asks, uncertainly. We have had supper, and it is beginning to get dark outside. Tash is sitting cross-legged on my bed. I *wish* she'd take her trainers off first! But I don't say anything.

'I don't know. Babs may have put him off. I'm not that bothered, anyway.'

'Hah!' Tash exclaims.

'What do you mean, "hah"?'

'You and your bikini.'

'OK, you're a fine one to talk! You couldn't take your eyes off him!'

There is a slight pause. 'What's that in your hand?' Tash asks me.

Reluctantly – I've just realised it's going to be hard to get any privacy around here! – I uncurl my fingers to show her the translucent pink stone in the palm of my hand.

'What's that?' she asks.

'Rose quartz.'

ROSE QUARTZ
'THE LOVE STONE'

'What's it for?'

'It's called the Love Stone.'

'Oh, I get it. It's supposed to make Gareth fall in love with you! What do you do – think of him while you're holding it? I notice you didn't offer it to *me*!'

'Oh, shut up, Tash! If you must know, I'm holding it so that you and I stop getting at each other, and start being friends again. We're not going to let some boy come between us, *are* we?'

Tash throws me with one of those sceptical, raised-eyebrow looks of hers – but her eyes are twinkling: 'Certainly *not*!' she says, hitting me with a pillow.

When we have finished pummelling each other with pillows, we lie back on the bed, laughing.

'I wonder what his star sign is?' I muse. 'He's *got* to be a fire sign – he obviously worships the sun.'

'And you worship *him* . . .'

I decide to ignore her – it's getting late, and I'm tired.

'I bet he's Aries,' I say. 'Yes, he's *definitely* Aries! Or he *might* be Leo – Leo's ruling planet is the Sun, after all. Relationships between Gemini and fire signs are always harmonious – apart from Darren. What are you reading?'

Tash has picked up a copy of *TeenScene*. 'I'm reading my horoscope,' she replies. 'It says, *Sagittarius is a shooting star, and sparks will fly when you meet your guy! Talk about love at first sight! Burn, baby, burn! Why not ask him out for a pizza? He'll love ya for it! Money matters continue to be bad, but Jupiter is about to align with Venus, who is entering her seventh house, and you won't be short of dosh for TOO long.* There! What do you think of *that*?'

ARIES – GARETH

'I didn't think you believed in horoscopes. They can be interpreted in all sorts of ways, you know – you shouldn't take them at face value. What does mine say?'

'I *don't* believe in them. It's a load of rubbish. Although it's a bit weird, don't you think, that reference to pizza? Anyway, here's yours, *Gemini is an air sign, breezing through life and flirting madly with every gorgeous guy you meet . . .'*

'I do *not*!'

Tash grins at me, infuriatingly. She carries on reading. *'But you are about to meet a guy who will blow you away! So grab him while you can! But be careful – don't get your fingers burned! He may be too hot to handle! Money matters are still bad – but the Moon is in its final phase, and your future should be looking rosy before the end of the month!* So, how do you interpret that?'

Still clutching my rose quartz crystal, I turn to Tash, and say, 'There's probably some truth in it, but let's just remember what's important – I mean, our friendship. I don't want to get my fingers burned. Love and money are important matters, but I don't want them to come between us. I want us to be Best Mates Forever!'

Tash smiles. 'Me too,' she says.

Chapter 11

Natasha

'BE–BE–BEEP! BE–BE–BEEP! BE-BE-BEEP! BE-BE-BEEP!!!'

'For God's sake, turn it *off*!'

Sophie has set her phone to wake us up, and left it on the other side of the room so that we *have* to get up, but she seems to expect *me* to be the one to go and turn it off!

I have woken up shivering, as Sophie has rolled herself up in the duvet, like a caterpillar. There is no sun streaming through the sun catcher or glinting off the crystals this morning – the sky is grey and overcast, and a thin, cool breeze is lifting the pink net curtain. I pull the window shut.

Sophie and I look at each other – it is almost scary how we can read each other's minds sometimes.

'He won't be sunbathing today!' we both say.

* * *

It hasn't taken me long to realise that things are different at Sophie's house from what I am used to. Despite telling Sophie's mum that I don't usually bother with breakfast – or I might just grab a cereal bar as I head out through the door – I am told very firmly that I must 'Sit down and eat a proper breakfast!' I am amazed at how many bowls of cereal and slices of toast Kyle consumes. 'He's a growing boy!' says his mum, proudly. 'He's a pig!' says his sister.

We hurry home after school to get changed before we go to work, and I struggle to bring my windswept hair under control. I envy Sophie her lovely straight hair. Sophie takes *forever* deciding what to wear.

'Don't bother, Sofe! By the time we get there, he'll probably have gone to the Pizza Palace,' I observe.

Sophie pulls a face at me. 'I'm only sorting out some different clothes because the weather's changed,' she says. 'And since when did you start wearing so much make-up? Hang on – that's *my* make-up, isn't it?'

'I didn't think you'd mind.'

'I don't, but you could have asked!'

For the first time since I arrived, I feel awkward. Sophie doesn't usually complain.

'Sorry, Sofe! I'll ask next time. At least you don't need to worry about me borrowing your clothes.'

This is true – Sophie's longest trousers would be

three-quarter length on me! And I don't see myself in her favourite purple skirt with the tasselled hem. This is what Sophie eventually decides to wear, with a matching Indian-style bag, hanging from her shoulder by a thin strap, and a short lime-green top which shows off her bare midriff.

'Not *quite* a bikini!' I remark. 'Can we go *now*, please, so we stand a chance of getting there before midnight?'

Sophie's mum has given us the key to let ourselves into Babs's house, so that we don't have to disturb her mother. She has also given us a fruit-cake in a tin, which she has baked specially for the elderly lady. Sophie's mum likes to bake late at night – she says that she finds it relaxing. Sophie lets us in, while I carry the cake. I nearly drop it, as Crumpet bounds up to us, barking joyfully, jumping up and down like a large, hairy grasshopper, and dashing to and fro around our legs.

Mrs Ames's mum – Sophie and I find it easier to think of her as Granny, although we call her Mrs Clarkson to her face – is delighted with the cake, and invites us to sit down and share it with her. I offer to make us some tea, and Granny accepts, gratefully. Her living-room has big french windows looking out over the back garden, and there is a bird table just outside. Granny asks us to put fresh bird-seed on it, and tells us where the bird-seed is kept.

Sophie keeps looking into the garden and craning her neck, as if trying to see something just out of sight.

'Did you see him, dear?' Granny enquires. 'Isn't he handsome? So beautiful! He visits *every* day. Such a fine fellow.'

Sophie is blushing. I am not sure what to think.

'My great-spotted woodpecker!' Granny exclaims, reaching down beside her chair and picking up a pair of binoculars. She lifts them to her eyes, and gazes out into the garden. 'I think he's gone now – but he'll be back . . .'

'You didn't really think . . .?' I begin, as I tip bird-seed on to the bird table.

Granny is smiling and waving at us through the french windows. Sophie gives a little wave back. Crumpet is dashing up and down the garden, chasing any bird that dares to fly too close.

'No,' she says. 'I *knew* she was talking about her birds.'

I empty the entire bag of bird-seed on to the little wooden table, and a lot of it spills off the sides – the birds can have a treat.

'She's really nice, isn't she – Mrs Ames's mother?' I comment.

'Yes,' Sophie agrees. 'She's the best sort of granny – they always have biscuits, and cake, and stuff. And they're always pleased to see you. Do you think she'd let us adopt her as *our* granny? Tash – stop looking into next door's garden . . .'

'I'm not looking.'

'Yes, you *are*! You're trying to see over the hedge – it's a bit obvious. Can you see anything?'

'No, I don't think he's there.'

'OK, so let's get on with our work – that's why we're here, isn't it?'

Yes, I *know* it is! But she was just as keen as I was to see him. She doesn't fool me . . . Sophie is so small and skinny – she looks about twelve years old in that tight-fitting green top. Why doesn't she get a padded bra? Does she *really* think that a bronzed seventeen-year-old Sun God is going to be interested in *her*? At least I'm nearly the same height as he is – and I think I look older than I am; I don't need a padded bra.

Crumpet takes us for a walk. Sophie hangs on to the end of his lead as he strains to get at lampposts, pillar boxes, trees, bushes, a passing cat (that freezes and arches its back, hissing) and anywhere he can locate a really disgusting smell.

Sophie and I discuss pooper-scooper duties. We

agree to take it in turns, but can't agree who should be first. Babs has already told us to use the doggy doo-doo bags she keeps in the utility room, and then put them in the incinerator which looks like an old metal dustbin, and is situated at the bottom of the garden. I comment that the very thought of doing any such thing totally grosses me out. With a sigh, Sophie volunteers to do it.

We go to the park, where Crumpet chases pigeons and some ducks, before we bring him – or he brings us – back to his house, and we give him his Fido-food, which he gobbles down at record speed, and then he curls up in his tartan-lined basket, hiccuping.

I do some Hoovering – there are dog hairs everywhere – and Sophie waters the plants before we both help Granny with a small amount of washing-up. She insists on washing while we dry.

'I do miss Babs!' Granny says, with a sigh. 'The house seems very quiet without her. But I've got Crumpet, of course. And it's so nice to have the company of two such lovely girls – I'll see you bright and early tomorrow! I hope I won't give you a fright – I may not have had time to do my hair.'

* * *

'Er . . . Sophie? This isn't the way home!' I remark, as Sophie waits at a crossing for the lights to change, and I run a few steps to catch her up. Where is she going in such a hurry?

'Oh, I . . . I thought I might grab a pizza on the way. I'm starving, aren't you? I've got a few coins at the bottom of my bag, left over from my last pocket money – and the fifty pence we got for that card!'

I raise my eyebrows at Sophie quizzically, and point out that the Pizza Palace isn't exactly on the way home – it's a good ten-minute walk into the middle of Southway, in the opposite direction to Sophie's house.

'Time to work up even more of an appetite, then!' replies Sophie briskly.

'And I don't believe you're starving, either – you just ate about half a fruit-cake!' I say, scathingly.

'Tash, you *know* why I want to go to the Pizza Palace! Are you with me, or not?'

We peer though the window of the Pizza Palace.

'He's there! He's there!' Sophie exclaims.

'So stop jumping up and down like an idiot!' I hiss. (She can be seriously uncool sometimes!) 'Shall we go in?'

'Well, we could just stand outside like a couple of idiots, if you prefer . . . '

'OK. And *please* stop staring!' I snap at her, having my own back. 'He'll think we're stalking him.'

We are shown to a table near the front of the restaurant. Sadly, it is not one of the tables which Gareth is serving. Sophie asks if we can change, but we are told that the restaurant is too full. We order a cheese, tomato and sweetcorn pizza for two.

Sophie keeps jiggling around in her seat, trying to catch Gareth's eye – she can see him at the far end of the pizzeria. I am sitting with my back to him, and I don't want to be too obvious by turning round and staring. That sort of behaviour is more Sophie's style.

'He's seen me!' Sophie exclaims. She waves. 'He waved back! Tash – he *waved* at me! I got a *wave!*'

I ♥ PIZZA ! YUM . . .

'I'm happy for you – although I notice he's resisting the urge to come and say hello.'

'He's probably too busy.'

'Sophie, *please* stop bobbing around like that! You're giving me indigestion, and we haven't even got our pizza, yet.'

120

The pizza arrives.

'Mmm . . . yes!' says Sophie. 'Yum, yum, and yum!'

'It's good, isn't it?' I agree.

Sophie giggles. 'I didn't mean the food!' she says.

We make the pizza last as long as possible and then Sophie takes our bill to the cash desk at the far end of the restaurant. I go with her. We say hello to Gareth, who passes by with a tray full of dirty plates, on his way to the kitchen. He remarks that he didn't expect to see us there, and asks us if we enjoyed our pizza.

'Oh, yes!' Sophie exclaims. 'I can't get enough . . . pizza!'

She goes red in the face, and drops her loose change all over the floor. I feel very hot, and grin nervously – help! Let me out of here!

Sophie's mum is not pleased that we are back so late. We couldn't phone because we spent all our money on pizza. Sophie didn't have her mobile, and my battery was dead.

'What took you so long?' Sophie's mum asks, as we hang the key to Mrs Ames's house on the hook in the kitchen. 'You must have been redesigning the whole house and garden! I was about to phone Mrs Clarkson, although I didn't want to worry her.'

I am feeling full of pizza, and I just want to go upstairs to Sophie's room, but her mum insists that we sit down to fish pie with runner beans from the garden, followed by strawberries and cream.

'I am going to get *seriously* fat staying with you, Sofe!' I complain, jokingly, when we finally get to flop down in her room. I am *so* full! (We still have to do our homework.)

Sophie isn't listening. She rummages in her bedside drawer and brings out a small, creamy pearl-like stone, which she contemplates, holding it in her open palm.

'What's that?' I ask. (Don't tell me – it's a 'Gareth-stone'!)

'It's a moonstone,' Sophie replies. 'It's an emotional balancer. I need to calm down or I'll put him off.'

MOONSTONE

I decide to keep quiet. I don't want to disillusion Sophie – she *is* my best mate, after all – but, as we were leaving the Pizza Palace, Gareth came back from the kitchen carrying two pizzas on a tray, and he winked at me – Sophie didn't notice – and I smiled back.

In my opinion, a wink is so much more SUBTLE and MEANINGFUL and SIGNIFICANT than an ordinary, everyday, run-of-the-mill wave, although, I can't help worrying, maybe he doesn't really like either of us. I *hope* he didn't think we were stalking him today. I think Sophie goes too far, sometimes – about a million miles too far, sometimes!

Chapter 12
Sophie

I AM STILL HALF-ASLEEP, as I stumble across my room to switch off my phone – it is seven a.m. Tash – the lazy lump – is refusing to get up! 'Come on, Tash! We've got to go to *work*! We need to let Crumpet out for a pee.'

Looking out of the window I see that the sky is still grey and overcast, threatening rain.

'Can I borrow your straightener?' Tash asks, in a sleepy voice. 'It's better than mine. In fact, can I have it? You don't need a hair straightener.'

'I *do*!' I reply. 'Sometimes I get this wavy strand of hair . . .' But I can see that Tash has a point – she has *serious* bed hair! It has frizzed up during the night, and is standing on end, resembling the bristles on an old broom. 'Here, take it,' I say. 'Your need is greater than mine – but I'll have it back when you've finished!'

* * *

It took *ages* for Tash to straighten her hair (she looks weird with straight hair – I think her curls suit her better!). Crumpet, who is delighted to see us, has to make do with a brief run round the garden. He rockets to the far end and back again, then sniffs round some bushes and does what dogs do. Granny has appeared at the window, smiling and waving to us. Tash suddenly disappears indoors to make her a cup of tea.

Great. I am just bending down to use the purple pooper-scooper, which Tash has just thrown out through the door, along with a doggy doo-doo bag, before disappearing again, when a voice says, 'Hello!'

Looking up, I see Gareth grinning down at me over the hedge. NOOOOO! Why *now*?!

'Er . . . hi!' It is hard to look cool when you have a purple pooper-scooper in one hand and a doggy doo-doo bag in the other.

'Looks like you're getting all the best jobs,' Gareth says, jokingly. 'Hello, Crumpet, you scamp!'

I grin foolishly. My mind has gone blank, until one solitary mad thought flips into the empty chasm between my ears: at least the pooper-scooper matches my purple skirt!

'Well, I must go,' says Gareth. 'I've got to get to college – I just came out to grab my football shirt off the line before it starts raining . . . See you!' He heads back into his house, leaving me standing as if frozen to the spot, still holding my pooper-scooper and bag of dog mess. The first few drops of rain begin to fall on to my head.

'Sophie! Hurry up!' Tash calls from the back door. 'We'll be late for school! You look really sick – it can't be *that* bad, getting rid of dog mess.'

(She should try it – she really should.)

'It's your turn tomorrow!' I yell at her, as I head for the incinerator.

I don't want to talk about what just happened, but as far as I am concerned, it is *her* fault that it did! She left *me* to deal with the dog mess *in front of Gareth*! (Although she wasn't to know that he would appear . . .) But I wouldn't mind if the same thing were to happen to *her*, tomorrow! I suppose that *is* rather mean of me. I have never had spiteful feelings towards Tash before. What is wrong with me?! My lurve for Gareth seems to be bringing out the negative side of my Gemini personality!

I keep falling asleep at school. I was up late last night finishing my homework and then my day started Too Early. It didn't start too well, either – that pooper-scooper incident will haunt me forever! I feel as if I keep making a fool of myself whenever Gareth's around. I *need* my moonstone, and it's at home on my bedside table. We had to rush to get changed and get to school on time. Kyle didn't help by putting a spider down my shirt just as we were leaving. I had to tear off my shirt again to get rid of it, and I am *still* shuddering.

I need my moonstone even more when Darren comes over to us as we leave the canteen at lunchtime to go to our detention (we are allowed to eat a chicken burger first), and makes fun of Tash's hair. The weather has been showery and windy all morning, and her hair has gone *pouf*! All that hair-straightening was a waste of time – she now has a shock of fluffy little curls. Darren says that she looks like a poodle. I tell Darren to 'Shove off!!!' Tash – and Darren – both look at me, startled. This is the first time I have stood up to Darren – and it feels good . . .

'Thanks, Sofe!' says Tash as Darren slopes off, sneering at us over his shoulder. 'But he doesn't bother me *that* much, you know – you *have* stopped fancying him, haven't you?'

'Oh, yes!' Almost . . . 'I don't need Darren any more.'

'*N*eed him? No one in their right mind *needs* someone like Darren!' Tash scoffs.

I am almost glad to get to detention. It gives me the chance to sit quietly and try to focus my thoughts and feelings – and do a rude drawing of Darren, which sums up what I think of *him*! Next time I see Gareth, I will be in control, I will be calm and collected, I will be the Embodiment of Cool, I will no longer be Pooper-Scooper Girl!

Granny is pleased to see us later in the afternoon, and Crumpet is wildly excited. After he has had his walk and FidoFood, Tash gets down to some serious dusting (*still* trying to get out of pooper-scooper duties!), and I go into the garden with Crumpet, and water the plants. (Crumpet waters them, too.) The rain that fell earlier today turned out to be only a light shower, and the pots are dry.

I can hear a football being kicked in Gareth's garden – it must be *him*! Every time I hear the soft W*hump*! as his boot connects with the ball, my heart goes T*hump*!

I can't see anything because nearly all the pots are on a patio at the side of the house away from Gareth's garden, so I edge around the corner, my heart thumping madly, hoping to catch a glimpse without being too obvious – and without a pooper-scooper in my hand! I am wearing a cool white off-the-shoulder top and a jeans skirt – understated chic!

A flash of Gemini inspiration strikes me. I pick up a

dingy yellow tennis ball which is lying on the grass nearby – it must be one of Crumpet's many toys – and throw it. Whoops! It has sailed through the air into Gareth's garden! (Just as I intended . . . cunning, or what??!) Crumpet goes crashing through a small gap in the hedge to chase after the ball, and I hear Gareth laugh, and call to him.

'Mad!' Gareth exclaims, leaning over the hedge and shaking his head. Does he mean Crumpet – or me??!

'Yes! Completely barking!' I reply, wittily. (But does Gareth like witty girls?)

'Barking! Ha ha! Good one!'

Encouraged, I try to think of another witty remark, but my mind has now gone blank, so I ask him when his birthday is.

'April 2nd,' he replies, looking surprised.

I knew it! He *is* an Aries! A fire sign. He asks me when *my* birthday is. I wonder if he'll send me a card?!

'You're very good with Crumpet,' says Gareth, changing the subject from birthdays. 'You play with him, clean up after him . . . Crumpet always knows who his friends are. Look at him gazing up at you – he loves you!'

Crumpet has brought me the tennis ball, and is sitting at my feet, his tail gently thumping the ground. I throw the ball down the garden, and he races after it.

'As far as I'm concerned, any friend of Crumpet's is a

friend of mine,' says Gareth. 'So, I'll see you later!' He goes back to his football practice.

I mouth 'goodbye'. I am dumbstruck, lovestruck – just plain struck!!! I am now officially GARETH'S FRIEND!!!

'Crumpet, I love you!' I exclaim, as he bounds up to me, the tennis ball in his mouth. 'You've brought Gareth and me together! You're *amazing*! You really are a girl's best friend!'

Crumpet drops the ball at my feet, and tries to lick my hands as I crouch down to stroke him, and fuss over him.

'So, you're Gareth's friend. Big deal!'

This is not quite the enthusiastic and encouraging reaction I was looking for when I broke the Amazing News of my Conquest of Gareth's Heart to my Best Mate – I suppose she's jealous.

'Don't be like that, Tash! We're just friends, that's all.' Although I can't help hoping that Gareth and I might be more than just friends, given time!

Tash shrugs, and says she doesn't care – but the atmosphere between us is strained as we walk home, have supper, do our homework and prepare for bed.

Kyle knocks on our door just as I am about to turn the light off.

'What do you want, Kyle?' I snap. I am tired.

'I came to say "sorry" about putting that spider down your shirt this morning.'

'You *should* be sorry! Don't *ever* do that again!'

'I won't. Listen, I couldn't help noticing – have you two had a row?' I open my mouth to speak, and Tash glances at me, but Kyle carries on, 'You should always say sorry before bedtime, you know – like I just did. That's what Aunty Aggie advises in her problem page in *Lurve* magazine.'

'Thanks, Kyle, but we're OK.'

Kyle regards us seriously. 'Being best mates is the most important thing, you know,' he says. 'You shouldn't let *anything* spoil *that*.'

'Is that what Aunty Aggie advises?' Tash asks.

'No, it's what Uncle Kyle advises.' He says this so seriously that Tash and I both start giggling. 'There! That's better!' says Kyle, and he leaves.

My brother is a weird mixture: frogs and spiders in the morning, and rare insights at night. The symbol for Pisces is two fish, swimming in opposite directions; just like the symbol for Gemini is the twins. We both have two distinct sides to our personalities!

I have trouble getting to sleep. I don't feel that things are right between me and Tash . . . and I'm too excited about me and Gareth!

Chapter 13

Natasha

TODAY IS SATURDAY, AND THERE is sunlight streaming through the sun catcher when I wake up, spilling jewel-like colours across the room through a gap between the curtains.

When I check my phone there is a message from Mum (it says, simply, 'LOVE YOU!' which makes me smile). I stop smiling when I realise that it is nearly eleven a.m.! Sophie must have forgotten to set her alarm (I'll set *mine*, in future!) – and we've overslept. Poor Crumpet must be crossing all four legs!

While we are scrambling around, trying to find our clothes (Sophie keeps nagging me about the mess, as if it is *all* mine, which it isn't), Sophie remarks that it doesn't matter that we've overslept because Gareth probably isn't up yet. This makes me angry, and I snap at her that Gareth seems to be the only person she thinks about, apart from herself. Doesn't she care about

Granny and Crumpet? 'And where's the new blue top Mum gave me?' I wail. Not being able to find it seems like the final straw!

We walk to Mrs Ames's house in silence, and find that Granny has fed Crumpet and let him out in the garden *and* cleaned up after him. She looks tired, and Sophie and I exchange guilty looks. Sophie offers to make her a cup of tea, and she accepts gratefully, while I go out to check the soil in the pots. Granny suggests that I water them later, when the sun isn't so hot. I wonder if I should mow the grass . . .

'Hi!' says a voice.

'Oh! Er . . . hi!' Looking round, I see Gareth, smiling at me over the hedge.

'Where's Crumpet?' he asks.

'Lying down indoors. I think it's too hot for him.'

'Not surprised – poor fellow! It's going to be hot this afternoon, playing football. Can you get that football for me? I kicked it over the hedge by mistake. It's over there, under the tree.'

It occurs to me that this is a golden opportunity to impress Gareth, and show Sophie that she isn't the *only* one who can be friends with him! I have an advantage – I can play football, and Sophie *can't*!

I fetch the football, place it carefully on the lawn a few yards away from the tree – I am aware that Gareth is watching me curiously – and line myself up.

My heart is beating fast, as if I am about
to take a crucial penalty shot. Trying
to look casual as well as supremely
talented at football, I kick the ball high into the air,
and it thuds down in Gareth's garden.

'Cool!' Gareth exclaims. 'You're good!'

Bursting with pride, I explain that I play for the
Southway All-Girls football team, and that we haven't
lost a match all season. I forget to mention that we've
only played one match so far this year, and that we only
won that because the other team scored an own goal . . .

'Cool!' says Gareth again. 'Do you want to come over
here and kick the ball around with me? Do you think
they could spare you for a few minutes?' He nods in the
direction of Mrs Ames's house.

'I don't think they'd miss me *too* much!' I reply,
smiling.

* * *

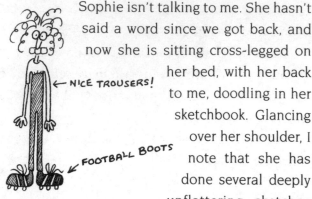
← NICE TROUSERS!

← FOOTBALL BOOTS

STICK INSECT WITH BIG HAIR

Sophie isn't talking to me. She hasn't said a word since we got back, and now she is sitting cross-legged on her bed, with her back to me, doodling in her sketchbook. Glancing over her shoulder, I note that she has done several deeply unflattering sketches of a stick insect with *big* curly hair . . .

'It's because I played football with Gareth, isn't it?' I observe, perceptively.

Sophie heaves a deep, long-suffering sigh. She still doesn't look at me. 'While you were fooling around with Gareth,' she says, 'I did the dusting, the Hoovering, polished the brass and silver, and clipped the hedge.'

'I know,' I say. 'I've never seen anyone clip a hedge so furiously. Gareth and I were worried there wasn't going to be any hedge left!'

'Oh! So it's "Gareth and I" now, is it? So you're an item, *are* you? You and your stupid football!'

I am shocked into silence for a few moments. Sarcasm doesn't suit Sophie. I tell her this. She tells me to get lost.

'This is stupid!' I shout. 'We said we'd never let a boy

come between us – remember? Where's your Calming Stone, and the one that stops you being jealous?'

'*I'm not jealous*! And I can't find any of my stones because *you've* probably lost them, because you spend all your time, when you're not chasing Gareth, messing up *my* room!'

We stare at each other for a few moments in horrified silence. Then I turn and run out of the room, down the stairs, out of the house and all the way back to my own home.

'Don't look so sad,' says Kezia, gently, passing me another tissue from the box on her bedside table. I am sitting on the bed beside her, and she has her arm around me. 'I miss Mum too – but she'll be back tomorrow!'

'It's not *just* that I miss Mum . . .' I tell Kezia everything – about Gareth, and Sophie, and the Falling Out.

'Ah . . .' says Kezia, nodding thoughtfully. She advises me to stop talking about Gareth in front of Sophie, and to concentrate on other things that are more likely to bring Sophie and me back together.

She tells me that it is more important, particularly at my age, to have a best friend whom I can rely on, rather than chase after a boy who probably isn't *that* interested in me. 'OK', she adds, seeing the expression on my face. 'I'm sure he likes you a lot – but maybe not quite as much as you like him.'

I know that Kezia means well, and I give her a hug. 'Thanks, Kez – you could take over from Aunty Aggie!'

Kezia looks confused – maybe she hasn't heard of Aunty Aggie . . . It's funny how my sister and Sophie's brother have become the Voices of Wisdom. Unfortunately, I am not sure that Sophie is in the right mood to listen to anyone's wise words.

Chapter 14

Sophie

SUNDAY. I WAS RELIEVED WHEN Tash came back yesterday evening, but I didn't want to let on that I was pleased to see her, since I am still upset that she went to play football with Gareth, and neither of them thought to ask *me*. (The fact that I can't kick a ball for love nor money is irrelevant.)

Tash tidied the room in total silence, found her new blue top stuffed under the bed with a lot of other things, including some of my stones, and then we went to bed.

Tash's mum gets back today, so I suppose Tash will be going home later.

'You look happy,' I remark, breaking the silence.

'I am. Mum gets back today.'

'Is that the only reason you're happy?'

'What do you mean?'

'Gareth . . .'

'Oh, for goodness' sake! You can be really immature sometimes, Sophie! Oh, I'm sorry! Forget I said that.'

Too late. How dare *she* accuse *me* of being immature!?! I'*m* not the one trowelling on the make-up *and* wearing very short shorts to go and cut the grass! Who's she trying to impress? No prizes for guessing!!!

Now we are NOT SPEAKING even more than we were NOT SPEAKING before.

Granny is as pleased to see us as she always is, and is thrilled with the fruit-cake that Mum has sent over. (Granny enjoyed the first one so much that Mum has baked another.)

She insists that we have some cake with morning coffee, and gives a very small chunk of cake on a plate to Crumpet, who gobbles it up, wagging his tail and sniffing around for more. She fondles the dog's silky ears. 'He's such good company,' she says. 'I don't know what I'd do if anything happened to him,' she adds, with a sigh.

In order to distract Granny from sad thoughts, I pick up today's copy of the *Daily Scandal*, her favourite newspaper, and turn to the page with the horoscopes. I ask Granny when her birthday is. She tells me that it is on December 2nd – she is Sagittarius, like Tash. I insist on reading their horoscope aloud and begin. Granny

HORACE VON STARGAZER

tells me that I will have to read louder, so that she can more easily hear the predictions of Horace Von Stargazer, the *Scandal*'s Number One astrologer! I am concentrating so hard on projecting my voice that I am not really paying much attention to what I am reading – before I can stop myself, I have blurted out that Granny and Tash will lose a much-loved pet in the near future, but that they will gain wisdom and attain spiritual growth.

Now I feel *awful*. Granny looks sad and worried. I meant to cheer her up – not make her feel worse, and Tash is mouthing 'Idiot!' at me – which doesn't help the way I am feeling. I stammer something about how you shouldn't take horoscopes too seriously (especially ones by Horace Von Stargazer!), but the damage is done.

'I . . . I think I'll go and cut the grass,' I mutter.

'That's my job!' says Tash, firmly. 'You can weed.'

I know why Tash wants to be in the garden – so that she can look out for Gareth! I am aware that we keep glancing at each other, and looking away again quickly, and we both keep glancing at the hedge (it is easier to see over it since I trimmed it!). I *know* this is stupid behaviour – but I *don't* know how to stop it!

There is no sign of Gareth. Granny comes out to ask Tash and me to go to the shop for her. I ask her if she would like us to take Crumpet with us, but she says that she thinks she will keep him with her for now. I feel doubly awful – I have really worried her! I *hope* there's no truth in the horoscope . . .

Granny rootles about in the large black handbag that she always carries around with her, even when she goes to put the kettle on, and produces a slightly crumpled list.

'I hope you can read my writing!' she says. My eye hits on Exceedingly Rich Tea Biscuits, milk and fishcakes. Getting out her purse, she hands me five pound coins. 'You and Tash are to buy some chocolate with the change!' she says, with an attempt at a smile. She is so kind – even after I upset her – although I didn't mean to.

Tash and I walk to the Minimart, which is open seven days a week, in thoughtful silence. Are we on the verge of Making Up? I don't think I can stand Not Talking for much longer!

But all other thoughts are swept out of my mind when we walk into the Minimart and see Kezia, leaning casually against the organic fruit and veg stand, talking to two boys, one of whom is very tall with short reddish-brown hair, dyed green at the tips. He has little round glasses, perched on a long thin nose, and is wearing dark orange trousers and a light orange T-shirt. He resembles a carrot, possibly an organic one. And the other boy is . . . Gareth!

'Hi, Tash! Hi, Sofe!' Kezia calls to us. 'Mum called this morning, Tash – she'll be home this evening – she's visiting Gran again. Look who I've just met!' She gives Gareth a playful push. She's FLIRTING!!! WITH GARETH!!! It's outrageous! She's even worse than Tash.

'This is Geoffrey, by the way.' Kezia introduces the Carrot, who gives a little wave. 'He goes to college, too – so we all know each other – but we've never really spoken before. I don't know why. Geoffrey's just bought one of your cards!'

But I have had enough. I am too confused by the situation to be really pleased that someone has bought a card. Muttering something about 'getting on with the shopping', I escape down an aisle with a basket and Granny's shopping

GEOFFREY

list. Then I realise that Tash hasn't followed me. Where *is* she? Sweeping the items on Granny's list into my basket, I round the corner of the aisle and am confronted by a scene which confirms all my worst fears.

Kezia and Carrot Boy have gone, leaving Tash and Gareth standing close together, apparently deep in conversation. Now I know that there is something going on . . . I feel sure that Tash hasn't been checking her phone for messages from her mum like she said she was – she was searching for messages from Gareth! IT ALL ADDS UP!

Chapter 15

Natasha

'*I DON'T KNOW WHAT YOUR* problem is, Sophie!' We are walking back to Sophie's house for lunch after delivering Granny's shopping. 'Aren't you pleased that Gareth has offered to roll the lawn for us? I told him that it was all lumpy, and the lumps show now I've cut it . . .'

'It looks more like you've *shaved* it.'

'Well, there are hardly any plants left after your "weeding"!'

Silence.

'And he's coming over after lunch to do the rolling, since you don't ask,' I say.

More silence.

We eat Sunday lunch in silence. We are late – I apologise to Sophie's mum – but she has kept some for us. Then we go up to Sophie's room, still in silence, do our hair and apply make-up (in silence), change into even skimpier shorts (in silence) – it is a *very* hot day, although Sophie's desire to flash her flesh at Gareth is as obvious as it is sad – and return to our work (in silence).

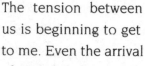

The tension between us is beginning to get to me. Even the arrival of Gareth fails to make me feel right.

'Hello, you two!' he greets us. 'I'm ready to rock and roll!' His smile fades slightly, as we both fail to laugh at his joke. I force a smile, and Sophie stares down at the lumpy lawn.

'OK,' says Gareth, clearing his throat nervously. 'Take me to your roller!'

Once again Sophie and I fail to react. Help! I *must* lighten up.

Granny calls to us from the back door. 'I'm letting Crumpet out in the garden for a while – the poor thing's been cooped up for too long. But you will keep a close eye on him, won't you?'

Crumpet races joyfully up and down the garden,

barking loudly at two fat wood pigeons that had the audacity to land in *his* garden!

'Don't worry!' Sophie calls back. 'We won't let him out of our sight!'

As we walk with Gareth down the garden, he pulls off his white T-shirt (which contrasts beautifully with his bronzed skin . . . BLING!). Sophie and I are suddenly alert and interested!

The garden roller is a rusty old thing parked next to the incinerator. Gareth flexes his muscles (sigh!) and heaves the roller slowly up the lawn. He is sweating. Sophie and I are mesmerised – it's like a heat from the World's Most Musclebound Man Contest! Sophie is glaring at me. What *is* her problem?!

'Haven't you got Hoovering to do?' she asks me.

'What, on a day like this? *You* do it!'

Panting slightly, Gareth stops, leans on the handle of the roller and wipes his brow with the back of his hand.

'Don't argue!' he says. 'It's too hot! Where's Crumpet?'

'Oh *no*!' I clap my hand across my mouth.

'What?' Sophie looks alarmed.

'I don't *think* I closed the gate when we arrived!'

Sophie gives a shriek. Jumping to our feet, we both race towards the gate – it is open!

'Oh my God! Oh my God!' I keep repeating myself, unable to think clearly. 'It's all my fault!'

Sophie is in tears. 'Oh, Tash – we *must* find him! It doesn't matter whose fault it is! The only thing that matters is to get him back, and I want to find him *without* worrying Granny. You remember what she said – that she didn't know what she'd do if anything happened to . . . to Crumpet.' Sophie's voice falters.

I nod, dumbly. This doesn't feel real. How could Horace Von Stargazer's prediction possibly come true? It's a load of rubbish! Or is it . . .?

Gareth nods. 'Sophie's right,' he agrees. 'It's good to have someone around who can think clearly in a crisis.' He gives Sophie a pat on the shoulder, but I can see that she is too upset to really be pleased about this. I certainly don't begrudge her Gareth's admiration. Suddenly, I don't care any more who fancies who – I just want to find Crumpet. It's my fault for leaving the gate open, and if Sophie and I hadn't been too busy goggling at Gareth and wrapped up in our stupid feud, one of us might have noticed that Crumpet was no longer in the garden, and this would never have happened!

Gareth asks us where we usually take Crumpet for his daily walk.

'The park!' exclaims Sophie, and so we all head off in the direction of the park, after I have checked in the house to make sure Crumpet is not there. There is no sign of him, and Granny is asleep.

After a long and unsuccessful search behind and under nearly every tree and bush in the entire park, shouting 'Crumpet!' at the top of our voices, we are all looking stressed. We ask passers-by if any of them has seen a dog answering to Crumpet's description – but no one has.

Sophie looks scared. I feel sick. How can I ever face Granny again? Gareth looks as if he is running out of ideas, and keeps looking around in an agitated manner. 'We're going to have to tell Mrs Clarkson,' he says, in a low voice.

'No!' I wail. Then I burst into tears.

Sophie looks as though she is thinking hard. 'Hang on!' she exclaims. 'Wasn't he wearing a tag on his collar – with his name and the vet's phone number on it?'

Gareth and I both look at her. 'So what you're saying' – Gareth speaks slowly – 'is that someone might have found him, and handed him in at the vet's?'

'Yes! It's possible, isn't it? We'd better find out. I've got my mobile . . .' She fishes it out of the pocket of her shorts.

'Have you got the vet's number?' I ask.

'No, I'm phoning Granny.'

'Sophie – no!'

Sophie waves her hand at me to shut me up. 'We haven't really got a choice,' she says. 'Not any more. Hang on! It's ringing. It takes her a while to get to the phone, especially if she's been asleep . . .' (Granny has her own phone, on a little table beside the window.)

My insides are churning unpleasantly, and I am going hot and cold.

'Hello?' Sophie says, sounding nervous and breathless. 'We . . . we . . . can't find Crumpet. OH! OH!'

Gareth and I are both frantically mouthing 'WHAT?' at her.

'He's been found!' Sophie exclaims, her tears of despair turning to tears of joy. 'We'll be back soon!' she says, speaking into her phone. 'We'll go and collect him. OK . . . yes . . . I'll do that.' Sophie ends her call. 'Granny had a phone call from the vet's!' she explains. 'To say that someone had brought Crumpet in – they found him wandering around in Willow Court. Goodness knows how he found his way there. And he's *fine*!'

I give a little shriek, and Sophie and I fling ourselves into each other's arms, and give each other the Biggest Hug!

'We've got to phone Granny from the vet's,' she says. 'And she'll confirm that we are who we say we are, and then the vet will let us take Crumpet home.'

'And I'm *never* leaving the gate open again!' I say, firmly. 'I *know* what's important now. You were really great, Sophie!' I tell her. 'Much more use than I was – I was just a panicking mess!'

Sophie shrugs, and smiles. 'I'm just sorry it took something like this to bring us back together,' she says. 'We're both a couple of idiots, as far as I'm concerned.'

'That's true!' Gareth remarks, grinning – and we chase him part of the way to the vet's. He easily gets away from us!

Sophie and I slow down to a gentle stroll. Before we catch Gareth up, Sophie whispers to me: 'There isn't *really* anything going on between you and Gareth, is there?'

I give Sophie a LOOK – but it isn't an unfriendly one.

'I'm so sorry, Tash!' she apologises. 'I *knew* you wouldn't go behind my back – but then my imagination went hyper.'

'Let's just forget it!' I suggest. 'I'm so tired of us Falling Out and Not Speaking – it's all so stupid . . . it's much more fun being Best Mates Forever! Let's concentrate on our job, looking after Granny and Crumpet – I don't *ever* want it to get that scary again! It should be fun working together, so let's not mess it up – let's do it for love *and* money!'

We link arms, and wander along happily. When we catch up with Gareth he is talking on his mobile.

'Yes,' we hear him say. 'I love you, too!' Sophie and I exchange looks.

'Bye, Laura!' Gareth says. 'Love you!' And he KISSES his mobile!!!

Seeing the horrified expression on Sophie's face, I . . . I . . . can't help it – I start shaking with suppressed laughter! I think it must be out of sheer relief that there is no longer a reason for us to Fall Out – Gareth has a girlfriend!

Fortunately, Sophie sees the funny side, and soon we are falling about, giggling. Gareth, who has no idea why we are laughing, concludes that we are completely mad!

Granny is overjoyed to see Crumpet, and the feeling seems to be mutual! Crumpet was equally pleased to see us! He seems none the worse – or any less bouncy – for his big adventure.

Granny is very grateful to us for bringing him home. I feel guilty, as it was my fault that he went missing in the first place! I tell her how sorry I am – and she tells me not to be silly! 'Life's too short!' she says. 'The important thing is that he's home and well – aren't you, boy?' She fondles his silky ears, and he pushes her arm with his nose and licks her hand. 'That Horace Von

Stargazer was only *half* right – Crumpet was lost. But then he was found again!'

'And Sophie and I have gained wisdom and attained spiritual growth!' I exclaim. Sophie gives *me* a sceptical look!

Granny sends us to the Minimart to buy some of Crumpet's favourite dog biscuits, and a ready-made chocolate fudge cake for us to eat with a cup of tea, in celebration. She also asks Sophie to exchange the milk she got for her – Sophie explains that she got goats' milk by mistake, since she was distracted at the time by her stupid suspicious and jealous feelings!

I want to tell Kezia about our eventful afternoon, and be at home when Mum gets home – so, after we've had tea, done the washing-up and said goodbye to Granny and Crumpet (Gareth left earlier – he told us that he was taking his girlfriend to see a film), Sophie and I go back to my place, only to find . . . Kezia and Carrot Boy in the kitchen! They are holding hands!

'We met by the organic fruit and veg stand!' Kezia exclaims, her eyes shining. 'Isn't that spooky? I told Geoffrey about the prediction! He was amazed – weren't you, Geoffrey?'

Geoffrey nods, smiling, and pushes his glasses back up his freckled nose.

Sophie looks taken aback – perhaps she really *is*

psychic! But I can't help thinking, she only predicted that Kezia would *meet* someone beside the organic fruit and veg stand. She didn't  predict that Kezia would actually go *out* with a carrot! But he seems like a very nice carrot, and I feel happy for Kezia.

'There's a surprise for you upstairs, Tash,' says Kezia.

I'm already running up the stairs, two at a time, followed by Sophie.

And there it is. The double bed of my dreams! I stand and gaze at it in a kind of silent rapture. There is even a new double duvet with a cool blue and silver cover. Then I throw myself onto it, laughing, and spread out like a starfish. Sophie sits on the edge of the bed, smiling. 'It's great, Tash! This is a cool bed!'

At this moment we hear Mum's car drawing up outside. I fly down the stairs, out through the door and give her an Enormous Hug.

'Thanks, Mum! I love you!'

'I love you, too!'

Sophie is allowed to stay at my house for the night, to celebrate my new bed – it is oh *soooooooooo* comfortable! I can be a starfish! But tonight I won't be a starfish – I'd rather make room for my Best Mate (*and* my Best Sister, if she wants to join us – she must have said something to Dad on my behalf, because he phoned to say that I can bring a friend with me next time I come to stay – and he will pay us *both* for any babysitting!). Sophie is sitting cross-legged on her side of the bed, sketching. Leaning across, I see that she has drawn two little people arm-in-arm, smiling, and she has written 'BMF' beside them.

'You and me?' I ask.

She nods. 'Best Mates Forever!' she says.

Putting aside her sketchbook, she picks up the latest edition of *Lurve* magazine, which she has brought with her. 'So,' she says, 'do you believe in horoscopes now?'

I raise my eyebrows at her, but maybe not *quite* as sceptically as I did before the whole 'Gareth and the lost dog' episode.

'So what's in store for me *this* month?' I ask. 'I'm not sure if I really want to know – but I have a feeling you're going to tell me, anyway.'

Sophie gives a satisfied sigh, and, lifting her magazine so that I can't see her face, she reads: '*Sagittarians will have a REALLY good time this month! Your*

Lurve Curve will go shooting up to the stars, and you will earn a lot of money so that you can go on a MEGA shopping spree with your Best Mate, and really SPLASH that CASH, even though you know that the best things in life can't be bought with money, and you'd rather hang out with your best mate than do anything else . . .'

'Sophie?' I interrupt.

'Yes?'

'You're making this up, aren't you?'

Sophie grins. 'Yes,' she says. 'But it's true – isn't it?'

BEST MATES FOREVER !

If you would like more information about books available from Piccadilly Press and how to order them, please contact us at:

Piccadilly Press Ltd.
5 Castle Road
London
NW1 8PR

Tel: 020 7267 4492
Fax: 020 7267 4493

Feel free to visit our website at
www.piccadillypress.co.uk